# Love & The Come Up 2

## By: Kellz Kimberly

D1115141

*I remember the first time I looked into your eyes and felt my entire world flipped.*

*June 2009*

## 1: Haze

"I can't believe that you got me all the way in Philly just to get some fucking cheese steaks," I complained. Philly wasn't that far out the way but to be going out there for food blew my mind.

"For real though," Zeke sighed.

"Man y'all acting like y'all have something better to do. Y'all know if I don't come back with this sandwich for Emanii she's not only gonna curse my ass out but y'all gonna hear it too."

"I don't know what you did to Emanii, but she's not my sweet little cousin anymore," I laughed.

"I ain't do shit, that's that baby she's got growing up inside her."

"Nigga you put the baby in her therefore us taking this long as ride is your fault." Zeke told him.

"This is a 'we' problem so stop trying to put it all on me. I thought we were in this shit together, my niggas," Drix joked.

I paid his ass no mind as I pulled up to Geno's. We all got out of the car and headed towards the door. Geno's had the best cheese steaks in Philly, and even though I wasn't trying to come out here, I damn sure wasn't leaving without at least two sandwiches.

It was summer time so all the hunnies were out trying to get into something or just trying to find their next come up. As we walked inside all eyes were on us but that shit wasn't nothing new. Young Savages weren't young anymore and we damn sure wasn't hustling the blocks. At the age of twenty Zeke, Drix, and I were doing big things and making money.

"Haze, you trying to pull a double, my nigga?" Zeke asked as we stood there scooping out the scene.

"Fuck it; I don't got no one waiting at home for me. Pick them out."

A double is something Zeke and I started doing after we graduated high school. We would pick two girls out talk them up then bring them back to the room. We would handle the girl we were with then switch up making that shit a double play. It might have sounded foul but shit, we're young dudes gettin' paid and just trying to live life with no strings attached. Well I didn't have any strings attached Zeke was a whole different story. In my eyes, I was single and could do what the fuck I wanted to. Love didn't live anymore, which meant these chicks didn't get nothing but pipe from me.

"Those two over there," Zeke pointed out. I looked in the direction of the two girls. I couldn't see their faces but their backs were looking right.

"While y'all play y'all stupid ass game I'ma go order this food before Emanii starts blowing my damn phone up," Drix said.

I waved that nigga off and started walking in the direction of the girls when Zeke told me to hold up. Turning around to look at him, I saw him on the phone going off.

"Lemon, get the fuck off my line man. I don't have to tell you where the fuck I be. If you're tired of me fucking other chicks then maybe you should grow some fucking balls and leave my no good ass."

I shook my head at Zeke cause that nigga was forever going through some shit with Lemon. I continued making my way over to where shawty sat.

"Excuse me ma, can I talk to you for a second," I said, leaning up next to her only catching the side of her face.

"That would be a second too much for you to waste my time," she sassed not bothering even to look at me.

"Didn't your mother ever tell you that it's rude to not look at the person you're speaking too?"

"No, she didn't!" she spat.

I reached out caressing her ass knowing it would get a reaction out of her. She was feisty and from her demeanor she wasn't about to let some random dude caress on her ass. Just like I knew she would, she turned around looking straight at me with a scowl on her face. The smirk that was on mines quickly faded as I instantly recognized who is was.

"Macy?" I questioned even though I knew it was her.

"It must've taken her a minute to realize who I was because the scowl she had on her face turned into a faint smile at the same time I pulled out my gun and pointed it at her.

"Haze!" she said with tears in her eyes.

"OH MY GOD HAZE NO!!!!!" Eniko screamed next to her.

She screamed out a little too late because the bullets had already left the gun's chamber. She had broken my heart making it only right that I break hers.

I had to give it to Macy she stood there and was ready to take that bullet like a champ. As bad as I wanted to shoot her, I knew that I wasn't going to be able to. Right before I pulled the trigger, I moved my gun up a little only missing her head by a couple of inches.

"Nigga, you might want to move that gun from out of my girl's face." The feel of cold steel being pressed up against my head caused a smirk to appear on my face.

"Nah playa, I suggest you get that fucking gun from my head," I told him.

"And if I don't?"

"Then your brain is about to be all over that window over there," I heard Zeke say.

"Rex, just put the gun down," Macy told the dude. "Eniko, let's go." Macy left from in front of my gun with Eniko following close behind her. I spun around to get a good look at this Rex nigga.

"We need to get the fuck out of here. Them boys 'bout to be here in a hot minute," Drix said coming over to where we stood.

"Count your blessing nigga cause next time you might not be so lucky," the Rex dude said.

"I'ma hold you to that," I told him then left out with Zeke and Drix.

As soon as we pulled off, the cops were pulling up. I said a quick thank you to my mother because I knew we got out of there in time because of her. As bad as I didn't want to think about Macy, I couldn't help it. Seeing her tonight had me ten thirty hot, for the past two years a nigga had to deal with losing his mom and losing his heart. That shit was hard as fuck and I still wasn't over it. Macy wasn't just my heart she was my fuckin' soul and the younger me needed her back then. I don't even know what happened to her, after I told her about my moms I never heard from her ass again. She just abandoned a nigga like I didn't mean shit to her.

I can't lie, seeing another dude call Macy their girl caused a feeling I wasn't used to, which was jealousy. I didn't know who that nigga was, but I was going to make it my mission to find out. Wasn't no nigga supposed to be with Macy expect for me. My pride and ego wouldn't allow me to be with Macy after her disappearing act, which meant her ass was supposed to be alone. My logic on the situation was childish as fuck, but I didn't care. It was supposed to be Macy and Haze until the day we die. We might have been young when we got together, but I still knew that our feelings for each other went deeper than the two of us could explain. She fucked up what we could've built so it was only right she deal with that shit alone. I couldn't be happy with her and she wasn't going to happy without me.

"That shit is fuckin' crazy. What are the odds that we run into Eniko and Macy out here? This shit has to be a set up or something," Drix stressed.

"I don't even wanna talk about that shit," I gritted.

"You don't have to talk about the shit; I'll talk about it for you."

"Drix, I'm not even trying to hear yo ass talk about that shit. Stop tryin' to gossip like a lil' bitch!" I spat.

Drix was the only one who got to experience that true love shit so he didn't understand how fucked up I was behind this shit. I mean he saw the wrath of that shit but he didn't understand how I felt about the shit on the inside. On the outside I acted like Macy leaving didn't faze me too much, but on the inside, a nigga was dying. It took me a minute to come to terms with it and now seeing her ass again didn't do shit but bring back pain I felt.

"Nigga, are you that fucked up about seeing your first love? Shit, the way you be running through bitches it's hard to tell that you even still care about Macy. That shit happened two years ago." Drix was lucky that we were in this car because I would've fucked that nigga up for the shit that he was saying.

"Shut the fuck up before I kick your ass out my fucking car. If I don't want to talk about the shit then I don't fucking have to. Leave that shit where it is or deal with the fucking consequences of you bringin' that shit up."

"Haze, get the fuck out your feelings, my nigga. I'm not one of your little bitches; when you talk to a nigga add some fucking respect to your voice. I understand you hurtin' behind that shit but fuck her, my nigga."

"Both of y'all niggas in here arguing like some straight bitches. Chill the fuck out with the bullshit," Zeke said, trying to mediate the situation.

"Nah fuck that Zeke, Haze wanna act like a bitch because he saw his ex. That shit isn't even that fucking deep. If anyone should be mad, it should be me. This nigga wanna go and shoot shit the fuck up forgetting that I have a pregnant girl at home waiting on her damn cheese steaks.

"Oh shit, you didn't get her food," I laughed, letting the argument we just had go. Drix was right the shit wasn't that deep.

"Nigga, you were in line all that time and didn't get her shit," I laughed.

"Don't laugh and act like we cool now. The girl behind the counter was so shook she started moving slow as fuck trying to make my sandwich. I told her ass forget it cause I see ole boy with that gun to your head and shit. You my bro so of course I was going to come to your rescue instead of getting my baby's food."

"Man, Emanii's gonna give yo ass the business behind not having her food," Zeke said.

"I already know but she will be ight. Who was that nigga anyway?" Drix asked.

"Macy's new dude." I shrugged.

"Damn," was all Zeke and Drix said.

They didn't even have to say anything else because it was what it was. Macy obviously wasn't stunting me so I damn sure wasn't gonna be in my feelings behind her ass. Fuck her and that nigga. Love was for the weak and ya boy was far from that. It's been fuck bitches get money since Macy left, and now that she's reappeared, the motto wasn't going to change. The only thing that was going to change was the number of bodies that popped up because I was dead ass serious about killing any nigga she fucked with. Like I said before if I couldn't be happy with her, she wasn't about to be happy without me.

## 2: *Macy*

"Who the fuck was that nigga, Macy?" Rex spat. When Eniko and I left out of Geno's we jumped into my car and rode around the block where Rex wanted me to meet him. Eniko stayed in the car while Rex and I were in his car.

"That was my ex," I told him, keeping it short.

I was still in shock that Haze had tried to kill me tonight. I never thought in a million years that when I saw Haze again it would turn out the way that it did. I mean I didn't think it was going to be all hugs and kisses, I just didn't expect for a gun to be involved. Him pointing that gun at me crushed me and turned me on all in the same breath. Just from his demeanor I could tell that Haze wasn't the same person that I left two years ago.

"You wanna be a little more specific. That nigga had a gun pointed at you and the only thing you can say about the nigga is that he's your ex? Nah, something else has to be there for the nigga to want to kill you."

"Rex, it's nothing we dated when we were younger and I ended things when I moved away."

"Yeah ight yo ass would tell me anything. What you won't tell me I will find out," he said.

"There isn't anything for you to find out. I'm telling you he is just an ex."

I leaned over kissing him trying to make him believe that what I was telling him was true. I mean what I was saying wasn't a lie either. When it came to Haze, I never really talked about him or how deep our relationship was.

"You trying to spend the night at my crib?" he asked, pulling away from the kiss.

"I can't, Eniko and I have to talk to our parents about us going to school in New York."

"I don't understand why you trying to go all the way out there to school anyway. How you just going to leave your boy like that?"

"Shut up, NY isn't even that far away and you can come and visit me whenever," I told him.

"You don't got to tell me that shit because I already know."

"Whatever Rex," I playfully rolled my eyes.

I leaned over kissing him one last time before stepping out of his car.

"I love you Macy and when a nigga threatens you that means they are threatening me."

"You don't have to worry about him. I promise you." I blew him a kiss then got in the car with Eniko and pulled off.

"We need to tell our parents about moving to New York for school tonight," I told Eniko before she could bring up everything that happened.

"I thought we agreed to tell them at the end of summer."

"We did but things changed."

"What changed? You seeing Haze."

"Haze doesn't have anything to do with this. After him almost shooting me tonight, I could care less about his dumb ass."

"Come on Macy you don't have to lie to me. It's okay if what Haze did tonight hurt you. I'm sure him seeing you tonight hurt him."

"He has no reason to be fucking hurt. I didn't try to kill his ass!" I spat mad she was concerned about Haze.

"No you didn't, but you did just up and leave him without an explanation."

"So dad wanting to move away is my fault? If I recall, the whole conversation came up because you tried to be buried alive with fucking Liam. So if Haze has anyone that he needs to be mad with it's you."

"Whatever Macy, all I was trying to say is that we just graduated high school so the college conversation could wait. We already lied to them about us applying to some in state schools and they're not too fond of you right now."

I rolled my eyes at Eniko because she was always trying to consider our parents' feelings instead of worrying about herself first. I guess she felt guilty about how much she put them through when Liam died. When we first moved to Philly, the way Eniko was acting got worse. She went from eating a little bit to not eating at all and never sleeping. It took about a year and a half of counseling for Eniko to bounce back, and I couldn't even really say that she bounced back because she was a whole different person now.

Before it would be nothing to get Eniko to go out with me and party, to the movies, and everything else, but now it was like she didn't want to do too much of anything. Whenever a dude who looked like he hustled tried to talk to her she would play his ass to the left quick. Erin had to force her just to go to prom. I knew death changed people, I just never guessed Eniko would change as much as she did. She was still my sister and I loved her to death, which was why I stuck by her side. The way

I was there for her is the same way I needed her to be there for me when it came to this college thing and our parents.

"It's not even them who's not fond of me, it's my father and I don't even care too much because I'm not too fond of him either."

"When are you going to let go that he made you move away from Haze? It happened two years ago. I think it's for the best that we moved. I mean look at how Haze just pulled out a gun on you. It's obvious that the game has made him cold. Can you honestly say that you want to be with someone like that?

"What you mean I need to let it go. I will never forgive my father for what he did. He took the one person that I love with all of me away from me because he didn't approve of him. If Liam wasn't dead then you would feel the same way I feel about being taken away from the one you love."

"I'm not saying that I don't understand how you feel because I do. My thing is how long are you going to continue to act out behind it. It happened two years ago and you are still holdin' a grudge about it. Forgive and forget Macy damn. It was puppy love and it's obvious that the love y'all once shared is gone.

"So I guess what you and Liam had was puppy love too then, huh."

"It probably was but me being so young I thought it was the real deal. I shouldn't have fucked with him anyway. I knew I didn't want to be with a hustler, but I went against my better judgement and because of it I ended up hurt and confused."

I shook my head at Eniko because she was trying to act like what she shared with Liam wasn't nothing serious because he was gone. Eniko could believe what she wanted to but I knew the truth. What she called puppy love I called real. Couldn't nobody tell me anything when it came to what Haze and I shared. If it weren't for my father Haze and I would probably still be together. For so long I hated the ground my father walked on, I thought him wanting to move was random only to find out that he planned on us moving before Liam even died.

When I came back from Haze's house that night, my father took my phone and snapped it in two. Two days later, we moved out of New York, it was the fact that we moved so fast that I knew he had it planned. I was filled with rage because I knew that Haze was blowing my phone up and I couldn't do nothing about it. Eniko was so out of it that she ended up leaving her cell in her old apartment.

Being only sixteen and losing the one that you love was hard for me, so I started showing my ass and doing just about any and everything I could to piss my father off. From sneaking out of the house late at night to letting my father catch me smoking weed, I did it all and everything in between. The only reason I started to change my behavior was because I wasn't only hurting my father, I was hurting Erin too. Erin was the mother I never had and even though she agreed to move I knew she only felt it was best because of Eniko. I put my bad ways behind me and just focused on graduating high school and getting into college. All the college I applied to were in New York, I missed my city something serious and I wanted to move back. Philly was cool but it wasn't New York. I even convinced Eniko to applying to all the same school that I applied too. We both got into Long Island University with full scholarships.

We accepted the schools offer way before we graduated. The only thing left to do was tell our parents our plans. They weren't going to be happy but there wasn't anything they could really say. I was eighteen and so was Eniko so technically we could do whatever we wanted without having our parents' consent. I was doing this for me and it was something they were just gonna have to understand.

"You sure you want to do this right now?" Eniko asked as we walked towards our front door.

"There's no better time than the present." We walked in the house and I didn't see our parents in the living room.

"DAD, ERIN!" I yelled out as Eniko and I sat on the couch. They both came rushing down the stairs as if the house was on fire.

"Is everything okay?" Erin asked.

"Everything is fine we need to talk to the two of you," I explained.

"If you needed to talk to us then you could've came upstairs. There is no need for you to be yelling like the house is on fire if you just wanted to talk," my father said.

I rolled my eyes at his dramatic ass and silently wished that he wasn't my father.

"I don't care how old you get I will steal beat your ass, Macy. Roll them big ass eyes again," he dared.

"Martin!" Erin said, caressing his shoulder. "Okay so the two of you want to talk, what do you want to talk about?" she asked, sitting down at the other end of the L shaped couch.

"Well it's not even so much that we wanted to talk we have something to tell you," I started but couldn't finish because my father cut me off.

"Macy Renee Taylor you better not let the word pregnant come out of your mouth. I let you get away with dating that Rex kid, but I refuse to be okay with you being pregnant."

"Martin! Stop jumping to conclusions and let her talk."

"Thank you Erin," I smiled at her. She winked at me then nodded for me to keep going.

"Eniko and I both applied to Long Island University and they offered us both full scholarships." I paused to see their reaction.

"That's great!" Erin smiled. "I'm proud of both of you girls," she said, standing up to give us a hug.

"I'm glad that you're happy mom because we already accepted their offer." Eniko beamed.

"You might as well call them and decline their offer," my father said.

"Daddy, I'm not declining their offer; I want to go to LIU. They have a great Criminal Justice program."

"So do some of the local schools around here. I don't want you in New York."

"Martin, stop and be happy for them. They got a full ride to LIU," Erin said, coming to my defense.

"I don't care what they got. Paying for college isn't an issue. She's only trying to get back to New York so she can be underneath that boy. I'm not having that."

"No one is worried about Haze, I've already moved on from him."

"I know and I'm not too fond of that new boy either," he gritted.

"You never even met him."

Just like with Haze, I kept Rex away from my father because I knew that as soon he saw him that was going to be a wrap for another relationship. Instead, I allowed Erin to meet him and that was enough for my father, which was good for me.

"Martin, you already taught her everything that you can teach her at some point you are gonna have to let her go," Erin explained.

"I'll let her go when I'm ready to let her go and right now I'm not ready," my father said walking away.

"I'll talk to him, again congratulations girls. I'm proud of the both of you and if you want to go to LIU then I will make sure that it happens." She smiled at us before walking up the stairs. I looked at Eniko and she just shook her head at me.

"Why are you shaking your head?"

"What is supposed to happen with you and Rex while you are in New York and he is out here?"

"I have that under control," I told her.

"Yeah, I hope so," she said before walking off.

I didn't even know why she was worried about Rex and I because she didn't care for him too much because he hustled. I just didn't understand her she didn't want to date hustlers but she didn't give anyone else the time of day either. I thought the whole not dating a hustler thing was phase, but she was serious about it. I never pushed her into dating anyone because I figured she would come around when she was ready. Eniko being ready to date never came and I just didn't understand it. The only date she had in the past two years was when she went to our senior prom with the boy from the debate team.

Even though I was hurt behind leaving Haze, I still tried to date just to fill the void where my heart was supposed to be. A lot of the relationships I was in failed because I could never give the person I was dating my all. The dude would want to be all over me and I would push him away. Holding hands was a no no when it came to dating me and when they would say they loved me I would either ignore their declaration of love or just reply with "that's nice".

It didn't feel right to tell another boy I loved them when I knew he would never have my heart. My heart remained with Haze even though we weren't together anymore. At the start of my senior year I was ready just to give up dating all together because it was honestly a waste of time until I stumbled across Rex. Rex was someone that I saw often throughout the hood and on my way to school. He was well known and respected throughout Philly. He was 6'3 and fine. Tattoos adorned his arms making it hard to see his beautiful caramel skin. He didn't have a lot of hair on his head but he had enough for his curls to show. Rex honestly came out of left field when he stepped to me. Meeting Rex was something I was never going to forget because the way he stepped to me was unforgettable.

*After my last period class, I rushed out of class and out of my school. It was Friday and I was more than ready to go home, change clothes, and then hit the mall. Eniko had to go to counseling today so I was gonna be riding solo. When I got to my car there was dude sitting on the hood of it. I looked at him instantly recognizing who he was.*

*"Do you mind sitting another bitch's car because I don't appreciate you sitting on mine?" I had an instant attitude and didn't care to hide it from him.*

*"Wassup ma, I'm Rex."*

"Honestly I don't care who you are, all I care about is you getting off the hood of my car."

"Why you so feisty, ma?" he questioned, sliding off the hood of my car.

"Don't worry about it."

"It's hard not to worry bout it when I'm trying to turn that frown upside down."

"That was corny as hell and if you look at my face instead of my body you would see that I'm not interested in anything yo have to offer." I rolled my eyes at him, clicked the button on my key ring to unlock my doors, and got into my cars. His ass got in on my passenger side and put his seatbelt on.

"What do you think you're doing?"

"I don't know how you drive, ma. I would rather be safe than sorry. From your attitude you not the nicest person and I don't need to die because you got a bad case of road rage."

"What do you want from me?" I snapped.

"I want your unconditional love," he replied like it was something I could just hand over to him.

*"Nah I'm good on that, love don't live here,"* I told him.

*"Damn you cold, ma,"* he said, shaking like he caught a chill. *"Who broke your heart?"*

*"Don't worry about who broke it because it wasn't you so get out my car."*

*"I'm not even going to lie I thought you were fine before but after seeing you with an attitude you sexy as fuck to me. I might have to piss you off more often."* He smirked.

*"Again, what do you want from me because I would like to go home."* I was agitated and I knew he could tell but he wasn't paying it any mind.

*"Who broke your heart?"*

*"Why do you care if you don't even know me? Matter of fact, who are you?"* I already knew who he was, but I wasn't going to let him know that.

*"I already told you who I am. The name is Rex and you right I don't know you but I know who I want you to be."*

*"Oh yeah and who is that?"*

*"My future."*

*"How can you want me to be your future when you don't even know me? I could be the coldest bitch alive."*

*"Then that would be perfect because I'm the coldest nigga you will ever meet. Nah on some real shit, I be seeing you around and I like what I see."*

*"Oh so you're not only a crazy person but you're a stalker too."*

*"Hol' up, I don't stalk shit nor am I crazy. You cute and all but you ain't fine enough for me to stalk you. I'm the type of nigga that goes after what he wants and right now I want you."*

*"Then how did you find my car and what school I go to?" I asked, ignoring the fact that he said he wanted me.*

*"Information comes easy to a dude like me. Now back to the question at hand, who broke your heart."*

*"Again, why does it matter?"*

*"Cause I need to make sure that I'm nothing like that nigga. I need to know who so I can show that nigga how you supposed to treat a queen, and more importantly I need to know who the fuck made you so bitter so I can lay ole boy to rest." A smile formed on his face and my ass almost fainted. I blushed slightly and tucked my hair behind my ear.*

*"That's smile is fucking beautiful. You going to tell me your name."*

*"I thought info comes easy to a dude like you."*

*"Macy, a nigga was just trying to be polite."*

*"Oh I see, since you trying to be polite do you mind politely getting out my car so I can go home."*

*"Give me your number and you got it."*

*"Use that info that comes easy to you playa."*

*"Ight. When I text just make sure you text back." He winked then got out my car. I headed home and it wasn't long after I walked in the door that I got a text from Rex.*

I shook my head pulling myself out of my daydream. Rex had been a good distraction from the emptiness that I felt inside but I knew what we had was coming to an end soon. We were already at the point in the relationship where he was saying I love you. I never lied to Rex I told him that I wasn't ready for the whole love thing and he claimed to understand where I was coming from. With me moving to New York there was no way I was going to be able to fall for Rex the way that he had fallen for me, especially with me being so close to the person who held my heart in the palm of their hand.

## 3: Zeke

Waking up the next morning my head was throbbing like I had been out drinking the night away. Turning to the left, I checked to see if Lemon was still in bed. When I didn't feel her body I assumed she had already got up to start her day. I was glad she left me to sleep in peace because I wasn't ready to deal with her mouth today. Lemon and I had an on again off again relationship. I didn't know what it was but my dumb ass always found myself back with her. It wasn't love that had me keep coming back cause I never loved her, at some point I just chalked it up to the sex because she did have some great sex.

I rolled out of bed and grabbed my towel heading towards the bathroom. I turned the shower up all the way, stripped out of my clothes, then stepped into the steamy shower. I stood under the water trying to relieve the throbbing pain that was coming from my head. Yesterday was some shit out of a movie but it wasn't nothing I wasn't used to. In the last two year Young Savages had really came up. We were running everything in Queens and Brooklyn. The money was cool but I wanted more, I was ready to become a distro. I haven't brought the idea up to the other guys because they seem content with where they're at in the game.

The game was never supposed to be a lifelong thing but the way the money is coming in right now I don't know if I could let that shit go. Cash ruled everything in this world and the more money you have the more powerful people see you. We were only twenty so opening up anything right now would be hard. It would be a lot easier when we turned twenty-one, which meant we had another year in the game set. When that year was up, I was going to bring to Haze and Drix about us being distros. If they were down then we would continue to get money together. If they wanted to step out of the game that would be fine too, but I was going to continue to get this money.

The throbbing of my temples let up some while I started washing up. I rinsed off, stepped out the shower and wrapped my towel around my waist. Sliding my feet into my Nike slides I head for the kitchen to get something to drink. The smell of breakfast food hit me like a ton of bricks before I even reached the kitchen. I guess this was another reason why I always went back to Lemon. Her ass could cook and didn't mind cooking whenever I said I was hungry. If it weren't for Lemon's sneaky ways and her nagging she would probably be the perfect chick. But in the type of profession I'm in I couldn't deal with the nagging or the sneakiness. I kept her at arm's length only telling her shit she needed to know. I may have trusted her pussy to help me get a nut off but I didn't trust shit else about her.

"Good morning, Ezekiel," she cooed, looking at me like she had something on her mind.

"Wassup." I leaned over and kissed her on the cheek before reaching over her to grab a glass.

I grabbed the orange juice out the fridge and sat down at the table. Not even two minutes after I sat down, Lemon sat a plate loaded with cheese eggs, home fries, steak tips, and French toast on it. My mouth water at the sight of all this food. I dug into the food not paying attention to Lemon as she rambled on about something.

"Ezekiel, are you listening to me?"

"My bad ma, this food had my full attention. Wassup tho?"

"I'm tired of you coming in the house at all hours of the morning like you don't have me waiting at home for you."

"Lemon, I never asked you to be at home waiting for me. You chose to move in just like you chose to wait up for me. You should already know that I work late hours and if you can't handle it then we don't need to be together." I threw the paper towel I used to wipe my mouth on my plate and got up to leave out the kitchen. I already knew where this conversation was going because we had it so many times before.

"How are we ever supposed to talk about anything when all you do is walk away?" she sassed, coming into the room behind me.

"I walk away because we had this conversation one too many times. I'm not with the repetition stuff Lemon, shit. You not even trying to have a conversation you just ranting and raving about some bullshit."

"If you would just consider my feeling then you wouldn't have to hear my voice. All I ask is that you come home at a decent time so I'm not up with a phone in my hand worrying about you."

"Ight Lemon," I told her just to end this stupid ass conversation.

"Okay cool what are we doing today?" she asked, perking back up.

"I'm going to see my mother with Emanii…"

"Oh then you can count me out. I'm not trying to be around your wild ass sister."

"Watch your mouth, Lemon," I warned her. I didn't care if Lemon was my girl or not, I refused to allow any person on this earth to disrespect my mother or sister.

"What, she is wild. Up until she got pregnant, every time I ran into her she would try and fight me."

"That's cause you got a smart ass mouth and you don't know how to shut that shit some time."

"I don't have a smart ass mouth; I just don't allow people to disrespect me. I wish you would stick up for me the way you do your mama and your sister." She rolled her eyes then sat on the bed with stank face.

"They my hearts man, that shit is different," I told her honestly. I looked through my drawer and pulled out a pair of boxers to throw on.

"And what the fuck am I chopped liver?"

"You're Lemon." I smirked, holding back my laughter. Lemon was looking for something I was never going to give her.

"We have been together for about three years Ezekiel and all you can say is I'm Lemon."

"First off we been together on and off for the past three years, that shit ain't no relationship. This shit we got going on is more like a friendship."

"Friends don't fuck!" she spat.

"Why you trying to stress our situation when you already know what it is, Lemon? Every time I end shit with you, you come back talking about how you miss me and shit."

"Then why did you let me move in with you if I'm nothing more than a fuck to you?"

"I don't even fucking know, man," I said, running my hand over my face.

I couldn't even tell you when the fuck she moved in. It was like one minute she was spending the night like once a week then her ass just never fucking left. I didn't say nothing about it because it was cool to have someone here with me. My mother was in a home and my sister was living with Drix. I had a three-bedroom two-bath apartment in an apartment complex and sometimes that shit got lonely.

"Then maybe I should just leave since you don't even know what I'm doing here."

"That's cool, leave your key on the coffee table when you leave out," I told her.

"Wait you're not even going to fight for me! Fuck you, Ezekiel!" she gritted.

"Lemon, chill with the fucking dramatics ight."

"No I'm not chilling shit. All I ask is that you stand up for me the way you stand up for that retarded ass mama of yours and your pregnant teen sister but that shit is too much to fucking ask, right?"

My jaw flexed listening to her talk about my mother and sister. I wasn't the type to hit woman but when it came to my mother and sister I didn't play.

"Lemon, I'm trying to keep my cool but you pushing my fucking buttons. I'm not gonna tell your ass again to watch your fucking mouth," I warned her.

"I'm not watching a got damn thing. You can say whatever the fuck you want and not think about anyone's feelings but as soon as I say some out of line shit you wanna tell me to watch my mouth! Fuck you Zeke and your retarded ass mama. The both of you can kiss my fucking ass!" she yelled.

"Since it's fuck me get the fuck out of my house, Lemon. You not happy here anyway so the fuck is you staying for? You holding on to something that's never going to fucking happen. I don't love your sour patch ass and I never will."

That shit I said must've triggered something in her because she started spazzing one me. She jumped off the bed so quick and started running towards me with her arms moving in a windmill motion. She hit me a couple of times before I grabbed her wrist forcing her arms behind her back.

"Argh!" she cried out in pain.

"I'm going to let you go but only if you chill the fuck out," I told her.

"Fuck you Zeke. You don't love me anyway so just kill me now!" she sobbed.

*The fuck is she talking about kill me now. I swear on everything this is the last time I'm fucking with her dumb ass.* I thought to myself.

"Look like I said I'm going to let you go as long as you calm down, ight?"

She didn't say anything she just kept sobbing. I let her arms go and she fell to the floor. I shook my head and headed towards my closet to get dressed. I threw on a pair of basketball shorts and a black tee, walked out my closet, and Lemon was still sitting on the floor crying.

I walked over her ass grabbed my keys off the dresser and headed out the house. If she was looking for me to pick her up and baby her then she should've known better. I wasn't about to baby her ass because she was in the wrong. Every time she came back to me I would tell her that it was nothing more than sex and she would be okay with it. Then out of nowhere she would start talking about her feelings and that's when we would have our falling out. This go round I wasn't letting Lemon come back into my life. By the time I got back home Lemon would be gone and that would hopefully be the last time I saw her crazy ass.

\* \* \*

"Why every time we come here you want to bring Ma a damn teddy bear? You don't think she got enough of them shits," I told Emanii as we stepped on to the elevator.

Once I graduated high school, I did exactly what I promised Emanii, I put my mother in one of the best homes that I could find. She would go see a psychologist three times a week and it was really helping her. She still didn't care to leave out her apartment too much, but she was at least talking again. I made sure that both Emanii and I came to visit our mother at least four days out of the week. Emanii would sometimes come by herself but I made sure that we came to see my mother together often.

"I bring her teddy bears for the same reason that you bring her flowers. It makes her feel better."

"But at least my flowers die eventually; your bears just take up room."

"Why are you complaining, Ma loves my bears," she said, sticking out her tongue. I mushed her in the back of her head causing her to take a couple of extra steps.

"I can't wait until I have this baby so I can beat your ass, Zeeky."

"Don't embarrass yourself like that, Manii. You and I both know your hands aren't a match for mine."

"Yeah whatever just open the door," she said, pushing me.

I laughed and unlocked my mother's door. Walking in, she was sitting at the kitchen table like she did often.

"Hey Ma," Emanii smiled, sitting the bear on the couch.

"Manii, when are you going to stop bringing me those damn bears? I'm running out of space to put them." I laughed a little and Manii cut her eyes at me.

"I guess I will stop now," She sighed, giving my mother a hug.

I passed my mother her flowers, gave her a hug, and pulled out a chair at the table with her.

"Manii, you look like you are bout to pop." Since finding out Emanii was pregnant my mother only really cared to talk about the baby. I guess she looked at is her getting a second chance since Esque died.

"Ma, I'm only five months. I still have a whole four to go until I get to meet my little boy," she beamed.

"I'm going to need those four months to fly by. I can't wait to meet little Esque." Emanii and I both looked at each other when my mother said little Esque but neither of us said anything.

"I can wait," I said to try and shift the awkwardness in the room.

"Oh shut up Zeeky you know you are excited about the baby," Manii smiled.

It took me a while to get comfortable with the fact that my little sister was having a baby. Drix and I came to blows when I found out Emanii was pregnant. It was one thing for them to be dating but them being parents was something totally different. Drix and I stopped speaking for at least two months before I realized that there wasn't nothing I do about her being pregnant.

"Zeke, you're not happy about baby Esque?" my mother cooed.

"Yeah I'm happy just as long as Manii still goes to college."

"That's not going to change. I maybe having a baby but that doesn't mean I have to put my dreams on hold."

I nodded my head because I was going to make sure that her dreams didn't get put on hold. We stayed at my mother's until she had to go see her psychologist. Getting in the car my phone started ringing back to back.

"Answer your phone because that vibrating noise is bothering the shit out of me."

"How is a phone vibrating bothering you?" I asked her.

"I don't have to explain it to you just know that it is so answer your phone."

"Yo!" I said answering. We were still sitting in the parking lot of the nursing home.

"Ezekiel, why don't you love me?" she cried into the phone.

"Man Lemon, we already had this conversation, ma."

"I just need to know. What is it about me that makes me unlovable?"

I took a deep breath as my temples began to throb again. This shit with Lemon was starting to get out of hand.

"Look it's not you it's me. I'm damaged goods, ma. You don't deserve a dude like you me, you deserve someone that is ten times better than me," I told her only to get a response from the dial tone. I shook my head sat my phone down then pulled off.

"I don't even understand why you are still messing with that girl. You don't trust her nor do you love her yet you continue to fuck her then move her into your house."

"I didn't move her in, her ass just never left," I corrected Manii.

"Do you know how stupid you sound, Zeeky? That girl isn't all the way there and you need to leave her sour ass alone. What mother names their child Lemon?"

"That shit is a crazy name," I laughed.

"You should've just got with Eniko when you had the chance. Even though I can't stand that bitch she would've been off for you then Lemon."

"Damn why she got to be all that?"

"Don't play with me Zeeky you already know why I don't like them bitches. It was like one minute we were the best of friends and then the next minute they fucking vanished. Plus, you know I don't care for how Macy played Haze. I look at him as a brother too and she did him dirty. Now the nigga don't know how to keep his dick in his pants because of her."

"You wanna know what's crazy…" I stopped because I started second guessing if I should tell her that I ran into Macy and Eniko. Since I ran into them Eniko had been on my mind something crazy. All day I have been trying to push her to the back of my mind but the shit was inevitable.

"Are you going to tell me what's crazy or not big head?"

"Nah, never mind forget."

With Manii being pregnant, I didn't want to get her all worked up. In the last two years Emanii had a drastic change. She wasn't that sweet little girl anymore. She didn't take no shit from no one and her attitude was always on ten. I don't know if it was because she was around me and the rest of Young Savages or what. But her ass could turn into a savage if you pissed her off enough.

"Don't do that Zeeky you know I hate when you do that."

"Hate when I do what?" I played dumb.

"When you start to say something then say never mind. That bothers me so much."

"Ight, if I tell you then you have to stay calm, cool, and collected."

"Just tell me Zeeky, you are starting to be annoying."

"When we went to Philly last night to get your food we ran into Macy and Eniko."

"Say that again."

"We ran into Eniko and Macy. That's why Drix didn't get your food because Haze wild out and almost fucking shot Macy. Drix didn't tell you?"

"No that nigga didn't tell me. He told me about some shooting in the spot but he didn't tell me why or who the person was. What are they doing in Philly?"

"I don't even know but that shit felt surreal seeing them."

"Fuck them bitches!" she gritted.

"That was Haze's thoughts exactly." I laughed.

"No seriously, how did you feel when you saw Eniko?"

"I was cool," I lied.

For so long the last words Eniko said to me would replay in my head day after day. Those words haunted me because on the sly I wanted nothing more than to love her, but when she looked at me all she saw was a murder. She made it clear that she held me responsible for Liam's death and for a minute I believed that shit. For a while I was beating myself up behind her words. It wasn't until we started throwing an event in remembrance of Liam a year ago that I started to let the guilt leave me.

"Come on Zeeky, you know I know how you felt about her. I may not have told you this but I admired you for how you didn't let the fact Liam was dating her get in the way of the two of y'all friendship. That was a big thing you did."

"I couldn't keep her on the back burner while I figured shit out with Lemon. If things were supposed to be with Eniko and I then she would find her way back into my life."

"Then maybe you seeing her last night is her finding a way back into your life. I know you felt some way about seeing her so you might as well just tell me."

"Honestly, a nigga was stuck. For so long the look she gave me at the funeral was exactly how I remembered her. I remembered her for the last two years as the person who had so much hate and anger in their eyes when they looked at me. Last night though I didn't see the hate or anger in her eyes when she stared at me. She was looking at me the same way she looked at me when we first met."

"That's deep," Emanii said.

"Manii, you already know Eniko was the one I wanted to be with back then. I just allowed the relationship I was in with Lemon to stop me from making that move. By the time I realized that Lemon wasn't where I was trying to be Liam had already stepped to me about Eniko." I was never jealous of Liam getting with Eniko, but I wasn't happy about the shit either. I don't care how real a nigga say he is he never gonna be a hundred percent okay with his boy dating the chick he wanted to be with.

"Well you ran into her for a reason so you might want to explore and find out what that reason is."

"I don't know Emanii because I'm not the same dude she met three years ago and I'm sure she's not the same chick. For all I know we might not even work."

"Everyone changes Zeeky; that comes with age along with growth. Look at Drix and I we both changed and at first we weren't sure if we were going to make through the change but when you love someone you fight for the love y'all share. We had to learn each other all over again and now that we have, we are better than ever. The same thing is going to happen with you and Eniko. You can't expect her to have the same mind frame she had when you first met her because back then she was fourteen turning fifteen. She's eighteen now which means you have to step to her on some grown man shit."

"I hear you."

"I know you do just make sure you don't bring that bitch around me."

I laughed because Emanii went from giving me advice on Eniko to calling her a bitch in a split second.

"You can't act like that, Manii."

"Yes the hell I can. You won't understand because they weren't your friends. Matter of fact them bitches were more so like my sisters and they just up and bounced like I wasn't shit. That's like if Haze and Drix just disappeared on you."

"Ight, I get it," I told her, nodding my head.

"Exactly. That shit fucking hurts and I would hate to have to beat their asses so I would just rather not see them bitches ever again."

I left that conversation alone because I knew exactly where my sister was coming from. Haze and Drix were my brothers so if they were to just disappear a nigga would be all fucked up. Sooner or later though Emanii was gonna have to see them because I planned on making Eniko mine. The way I saw it she was supposed to be mine from jump. I know it sounded fucked up that I got feelings for my dead best friend's girl but it is what it is. Seeing her last night made my heart skipped more than few beats. Fate had it to where I would run into her two years after everything happen and that shit meant something. This time around I was going to make sure I handled thing accordingly because I wasn't about to lose out on her twice.

## *4: Eniko*

*"Work them hips slowly for me Eniko. I want to feel all of you," he moaned out.*

*I cupped my breast and rocked my hips nice and slow like he asked. We had been sexing a little over an hour with me experiencing multiple orgasms. I didn't think my body could take anymore but as I rocked back and forth and he caressed my nipples I felt my body ready to erupt.*

*"Cum with me," he cooed sexually.*

*I pressed my chest up against his and kissed him deeply. His tongue slipped in and out of my mouth as I slowly sucked on his lip. My body began to tremble as I felt myself reaching my peak.*

*"Cum with me, please!" I begged.*

*He gripped my hips holding them in place then exploded inside of me. I bite into the side of his neck because the pleasure was too much. We were both panting trying to steady our breathing as we basked in our sexual bliss.*

*"I love you Eniko. You know that, right?" he whispered into my ear.*

*"I love you too, Liam." I lifted my head from out of the crook of his neck and stared into his eyes, only they weren't the eyes that belonged to Liam.*

"OH MY GOD EZEKIEL!" I shouted, jumping out of my sleep. I touched all over my body to make sure that what just happened was in fact a dream. My hands slipped to my honey pot and it was dripping wet. I got out of my bed feeling uncomfortable from the dream I just had.

I changed out of my panties and threw on some clean ones along with a pair of shorts and headed straight for Macy's room. Walking in Macy's room, she was still asleep so I shook her to wake her up.

"Macy, get up," I told her.

"Just give me five more minutes," she groaned, turning over.

"Macy, I need you now," I told her.

"Fine Eniko damn, what's wrong?"

"I just had a sex dream about Zeke," I told her. The words escaped my mouth and guilt washed over me.

"Okay what's so bad about that?" she asked with the stupidest look on her face.

"I just had a sex dream about my dead boyfriend's best friend, Macy. That shit is wrong on so many levels," I told her.

"It's not like you actually had sex with him so you are good. Is that all because I kind of want to go back to sleep."

"No that's not all do you really think this move back to New York is the right thing to do?"

"From the way my father is talking we aren't going to be able to go anyway. Why wouldn't it be a good idea, LIU is a very good school."

"It's not about the school, you know if we go back to New York we are gonna run into Emanii. I can only imagine how she must feel about us and how we just left her for dead."

"We didn't really leave her for dead Emanii you were goin' through stuff and so was I…" Macy kept talking but I tuned her out because nothing she was saying was making me feel better about running into her. Just thinking about her brought back the memory of when I tried to call her.

*Sitting on in this room was starting to get the best of me. I have been going to counseling for the past two weeks since we moved to Philly. For the most part it helped but as soon as I left the office I would start feeling depressed all over again. Most days I stayed in my bedroom because there wasn't much else for me to do. My mother and Martin were always* asking me if I was okay, making it hard to talk to them. Macy was just as depressed as I was so talking to her wasn't going to make things better either. With my phone in my hand I thought about reaching out to Emanii. Without realizing it when we moved I left my phone in the house and Macy's phone was broke. My mother got me a new phone and on so many days I thought about dialing Emanii's number but when it was time to press dial I would chicken out.

Today was going to be a new day and today I was going to call my friend because I needed her right now. I dialed the number and when it was time to press the send button my hand trembled. I was nervous as if I was pulling the trigger of a gun. I wiped my forehead, then pressed the send button. The phone rang and rang and rang. The voicemail came on and that's when the tears started flowing down my eyes. Just hearing her voice was a little too much for me. I quickly hung up the phone before a message could be recorded and just sat there crying. Hearing her voice brought back everything that I have been through in the last year. From me gaining a sister, to me falling in love, to me feeling like my heart was being ripped out of my chest. It was just too much.

"Why are you crying?" Macy asked coming to my room and sitting on my bed.

*"I tried to call Emanii and when her voicemail picked up I heard her voice and just broke down. I need a friend right now Macy but I can't bear to hear her talk."*

*"I tried to call her too from the house phone when my dad and Erin wasn't here, I couldn't do it either. She's Haze's cousin so talking to her is only going to make me want to ask about him and asking about him isn't going to do nothing but drag me into a deeper depression."*

*"What are we going to do? I feel bad about leaving without saying anything to her."*

*"It's natural to feel bad but there is nothing that we can do. She is like a trigger for our pain because of whom she is connected to. Neither one of us is in the right space to where we can talk to her without thinking about Haze or Liam. Not talking to her may not be the right thing to do but talking to her and causing ourselves hurt and pain isn't the right thing to do either. We have no choice but to go on with our lives because my father isn't going to move us back to New York. We're just not in there emotionally yet."*

"Eniko are you even listening to me because if not I'm going back to sleep," she said, pulling the cover over her head.

I was glad that she said that because I could feel the tears starting to well up in my eyes. That memory was one that always stuck with me because I honestly felt like it was either I hurt Manii or I hurt myself. Macy and I made the selfish decision to hurt her because neither one of us could endure anymore hurt. Looking at the cable box I saw what time it was then turned back to Macy wondering why she was still trying to sleep.

"Macy, it's two in the afternoon wake up," I told her.

"Why are you waking me up? We don't have anything to do today. I just want to sleep the day away." She sighed.

"What's wrong? Is it because you ran into Haze last night? I know you brought up the whole college situation because you didn't want to talk about it but holding your feelings in isn't going to fix things."

"All those old feelings that I thought I suppressed for Haze came flooding back. I mean I never stopped loving him or anything; it just hit me hard as hell. He wasn't the same person that I knew and I think that's what's fucking me up the most, because I have a feeling I'm the reason why he is the way that he is. When I looked in his eyes all I saw was darkness and death. Do you know how crazy it was to see darkness and death in his eyes when I used be the one to bring out the love in them?"

"I didn't know it was that deep," I told her, sitting next to her on the bed.

"Yeah it is. We were young Eniko and I get that, but there wasn't nothing young about our love though. That shit was real."

A couple of tears dropped from her eyes, but she quickly wiped them away. Since we moved, Macy had become less in tune with her emotions. She never wanted to show weakness and put on this hard exterior. I didn't understand but I do now. Losing the person, she loved with all of her heart caused her to shut off any emotions she may have, because she didn't want to go through the same heartbreak twice.

I went to say something to her but my mother knocking the door stopped any conversation we were about to have.

"Come in!" Macy called out.

"I made lunch since the two of you never came down for breakfast. Your father and I would like to have a conversation with the two of you so throw on some clothes and come down," she said then closed the door.

"I wonder what they want to talk about?" Macy asked.

"We won't know if we stay up here," I told her.

"I'll meet you down there. I just gotta wash my face and brush my teeth first."

"So do I," I told her, leaving out of her room. I went into the bathroom washed my face, brushed my teeth, then headed downstairs.

My mother had cooked us meatball grinders and the sight of it had my mouth watering. I sat at the table not saying anything to my mother or Martin. When Macy came down this weird tension filled the room. It was so thick a knife wouldn't be able to cut through it.

"Okay now that we are all here we might as well talk before we eat lunch. After hearing what the two of you had to say last night about going to LIU, Martin and I had a talk. We think we found a solution that will make everyone happy, right Martin."

"Y'all want to go to LIU and I'm completely against that but Erin helped me to realize that y'all are not little girls anymore and I can't treat you as such. So this is my compromise, I'll allow the two of you to move back to New York for the summer and y'all can stay in Erin's old house."

"What's the catch?" I asked because this was too good to be true.

Martin wasn't my father, but he was hard on me the same way he was Macy. I may have been the best behaved out of the two of us, but letting us stay in New York by ourselves was something I just didn't see it happening.

"There is no catch. This is a test to see if the two of you can be in New York alone without getting in trouble. We won't be there to stop y'all from making bad decisions it will all be on you. The both of you have to get jobs and also pay us rent and buy food. Y'all want to be grown well now the two of you can be. If this whole summer goes by and y'all do what y'all need to do, then I will be okay with you staying there and going to LIU."

Macy and I looked at each other with the biggest smiles on our face before jumping on our parents giving them a hug.

"Don't hug us just yet. The two of you also have to find a way to move y'all stuff back to New York," my mother added in.

"Okay," Macy smiled, pulling out her phone. I already knew she was texting Rex asking him to help us move.

"Oh and no boys can spend the night at the house either," Martin added in snatching Macy's phone away from her.

"Dad!" she whined.

"Dad nothing, I want to make sure that you hear what I'm saying Macy. I'm not allowing you to move back so you can get caught back up in that boy. I'm letting you go because I'm trusting that everything I taught you has stuck with you and you are capable of making good decisions."

"Dad, I am more than capable of making good decisions not just in life but in my love life too. You taught me my worth and so much more," Macy told her father.

"Yeah okay Macy, I'm serious. Eniko you too," he said, looking at me sternly.

"I hear you, Martin. You don't have nothing to worry about."

"I hope not because your mother and I will not be available this summer."

"Wait, where are the two of you going?" I questioned with an eyebrow raised.

"We are going to do some traveling. Nothing too serious because we will still be in the states," my mother smiled.

My mother and Martin continued talking about all the places they planned on going and I couldn't have been happier for them. I was happy because my mother was finally starting to live her life after having me at such a young age. Most importantly, I was happy because I was about to be living on my own and it wasn't going to get any better than that.

* * *

"Eniko, when you going to stop playing with me and give me a chance?" Gavin asked walking up behind me and sliding his arms around my waist.

"Why would I give you a chance when you live in Philly and I'm going to be living in New York?" Gavin was Rex's best friend and he was fine as hell. He was tall, tatted, and had the prettiest green eyes I ever seen. The only problem was that he was in the streets heavy. After going through what I went through with Liam's death, I promised myself that I would never date another dude that was in the streets. I just couldn't see myself experiencing what I went through twice nor did I want to worry about him dying when he was out on the block either.

"Distance ain't shit when it comes to you. I would climb Mount Everest if you were at the top of it."

"You would climb that mountain for me?" I questioned, moving out of his embrace.

"Freezing my balls off and all, ma." I smiled at him blushing a little bit. Gavin was cool as hell and sometimes when Macy would go out with Rex I would tag along and chill with Gavin.

"That's nice to know but I'm not looking to date anyone right now," I told him.

"Why not?"

"That's not something I want to talk about either."

"I just moved all this shit for you, Eniko. You better tell me something." I laughed because I never asked him to help with moving our stuff, he just showed up and I wasn't about to tell him we didn't need the help.

"You chose to help with us moving. I never asked you to do that."

"What kind of dude would I be if I didn't do that for you? All I'm asking is for you to be real and tell me what's stopping you from fucking with me. We've kicked it more than a few times and our vibe is crazy so I know you feeling the kid. I just don't understand why you won't fuck with me one on one."

I bite my lip as he talked because everything he said was the truth. We vibe really well together and like I said before he was fine. I just couldn't allow myself to go down the same road with him that I did with Liam.

"You are into some things that I don't agree with. I already dealt with that and I'm not trying to go down that same path again because I don't think my heart can take it."

"Just cause you went down one path with one dude doesn't mean that you are going to go down the same path with me. I don't know who dude was but I can bet that nigga wasn't close to be doing the type of dude that I am."

"I hear what you're saying but I still feel the same way."

"What is it that I do that you don't agree with?"

"You're a hustler and that's something I can't get with."

He laughed at me then shook his head, confusing the shit out of me. "What's so funny?"

"Nothing ma. You're good, Eniko. You don't wanna mess with me right now and I'm cool with that. I'm not going to stop trying tho cause you something worth waiting for even if I have to wait my whole life."

He grabbed my hand pulled me towards him then kissed me on the forehead. He walked away from me heading back into the truck. I stood there feeling caught up with what just happened.

"Eniko, come upstairs so we can start putting stuff away. Why you just standing there like that?" Macy asked, standing next to me.

"Nothing," I told her.

"Alright well come on because we supposed to be going out with Rex and Gavin later."

"Wait what? I thought they were going back to Philly today."

"Nope Rex wants to stay in New York for a few days."

"Oh," I told her then followed her in the house.

Gavin being in New York for a couple of days meant that I was gonna have to be around him and that was something I didn't want. It was bad enough that I was back in the city, which meant I was bound to run into Zeke at some point, but to have Gavin here too was only going to make things more complicated. Gavin said he wasn't going to give up on me and even though that was cute I wish he would leave me alone. Then when I Zeke and I locked eyes back at Geno's it was like he silently said the same thing to me. I didn't need either one of them trying to get with me because as long as they both were in the streets I just couldn't do it. These streets didn't love nobody so I damn sure wasn't going to love anyone that was in the streets.

# 5: Emanii

Being pregnant at the age of eighteen wasn't the worse thing in the world but it wasn't the most ideal situation either. I had my whole life planned out to the T and getting pregnant damn sure wasn't a part of that plan. I couldn't complain though because I was sexing without protection like I was grown, so now I had to handle this pregnancy like I was grown. Things with Drix and I have been amazing since he told me about the shit his mother had him doing. Still to this day it was hard for me to believe that his mom was pimping him. I just couldn't for the life of me understand why or how a mother could do such a thing.

Drix and I didn't have to worry about that anymore because his mother was no long breathing. The way everything went down was so crazy because the same day his mother died was the same day that we made love for the first time. My eyes began to water as I reminisced about catching my first body and losing my virginity a year and a half ago.

*"I can't take this shit, Emanii!" Drix gritted as soon as I opened the front the door for him. He had called me an hour earlier asking if I was home alone because he wanted to come through. I told him that Zeke was out somewhere with one of his many bitches and for him to come.*

"What's wrong, Drix? You're shaking and it's scaring me." I pulled him over to the couch and wrapped my arms around him trying to get him to calm down.

"She's still fucking with me, Emanii," he mumbled.

"Tell me what's going on so I can help you Hendrix. I'm here for you just tell me what's going on!" I pleaded.

"When I get home last night I go into her room to give her the money that I owed her. As I was walking out she stopped me and said that she had a date for me. Now I had just paid her, which meant there shouldn't have been any fucking dates. She started talking about how she know what I'm out here doing and shit and that if me and my friends wanted to stay out of jail then I would go on the date that she has lined up for me. The fuck am I supposed to do, Emanii? I can't go another date. I'm finally in a space where I'm cool and shit. Going on a date ain't going to do nothing but fuck up my mental. Then on the other hand it's like how can I not go on the date cause I'm not about to let my boys get caught up because of me."

At first I couldn't even find the words to say to him. I couldn't tell him to go on the date because that would fuck him up but at the same time if he didn't that would be putting my brother and cousin in a fucked up situation. I kept my arms *wrapped around him as I tried to figure out a situation and the longer I thought about it the deeper my hatred for his mother grew. Then that's when it all clicked for me.*

*"We have to kill her, Drix," I whispered.*

*"What?" he asked, moving from out of my arms.*

*"We have to kill her that's the only way to stop her. Yeah, you are eighteen now but she has something that she can hang over your head."*

*"I'm not about to tell Haze and Zeke that I wanna kill my moms, then I'm have to explain why I'm killing her ass."*

*"You don't have to tell them nothing."*

*"I can't just kill her alone, Emanii."*

*"I can help you." I looked in his eyes to let him know just how serious I was.*

*"Ain't no way I'm going to take you to kill my fuckin' mother. I'll do the shit alone before I take you with me!" he spat, jumping up from the couch. He started pacing back and forth while shaking his head.*

*"You can't do it by yourself, Drix. You need me so let me be there for you."*

*"I said fucking no, Emanii. I'll handle this shit myself. I can't put you in danger behind my shit. Zeke won't ever let me live the shit down if something happens to you."*

*"And how am I supposed to feel if something happens to you or Zeke. No matter how you play this, one of you are going to get hurt. I can't just sit back knowing what's going on and not doing nothing. We are going to handle this together and that's the end of it!"*

*"Emanii, I said fucking no!"* My little ass jumped up so fast and slapped the shit out of him.

*"All your life you had to deal with this shit alone, I'm about to let you deal with it alone anymore. I will help you get through this and then we will move on from the shit together."*

I could tell that he wasn't happy about me helping him but he didn't have much of a choice. We waited until three in the morning that night to go back to his house and do the deed. At seventeen I caught my first body and that shit was exhilarating. Zeke had taught me how to use a gun after Liam died, but shooting at a piece of paper and actually shooting a person did something to me. It wasn't a good feeling but it wasn't a bad feeling either. It made me feel powerful. After that we cleaned up our mess then Drix and I went to a hotel and made love way into the morning.

"Come on Manii, I told you to be ready by one so we can get the wings and I can bring you back here cause I got a meeting at five," Drix complained.

"Drix, your meeting is at five it's only twelve thirty stop being dramatic." I waved him off. I was lying in bed with my towel on just waiting to get dressed. I wasn't one of them girls that took an hour to get ready. I literally threw on some clothes did my hair and was out the door.

"Come on ma, I'm hungry as shit."

"Fine you big baby." I giggle because Drix had been getting all my pregnancy cravings so far. I was five months in and my pregnancy was going smoothly. Drix was the one who got all the morning sickness and cravings.

"I'll be in the car. Hurry too," he said, kissing me before walking out the room.

I rolled out of bed sighing because I hated the summer with a passion. Granted I was born in July, I just hated how hot it was. I couldn't stand the heat and usually only left the house around five in the afternoon. I went over to my closet pulled out a sky blue high low dress and a pair of sandals. Laying it out on the bed I went to my vanity to do something with my hair. My hair had been growing crazy being pregnant and I was ready to cut it all off. It was curlier than normal and just a lot to deal with. I brushed the front part of it into a bun then left the back to hang out. I slipped the dress on, slid into my sandals, sprayed some perfume, and then I was out the door and in the car.

"I thought I was gonna have to come back in the house and drag your ass outside."

"I didn't even take long shut up. What is the meeting about that you have to go to?"

"Come on I already told you before that what happens in the game stays in the street. I'm not bringing that shit to our home or getting you involved. The less you know the better."

"I just don't understand why you can't just keep me in the know. You got Rose and her bimbos cooking for y'all but I can't know what's going on."

"Emanii, you not knowing is for your own good. If shit hits the fan you can't get jammed up cause you don't know shit."

"I wouldn't get jammed up because I know how to play dumb. It's not like I don't know that you are selling drugs."

"Knowing I'm out here selling drugs and knowing what I'm actually out here doing are two different things. You know the watered down version of what's going on and that's how that shit is going to say. End of discussion."

I rolled my eyes because this wasn't the end of the discussion by far. All I wanted was to know what was going on. I hated being left in the blind because if some shit popped off I wouldn't even know where to start to try and figure things out. This is why so many things went wrong in the game because the men felt leaving their girl in the blind was the best thing for them. Leaving me in the blind was the worst possible thing that could happen. They gave me a gun thinking that was supposed to protect me when they aren't around but what good is a gun if I don't even know who my own enemies are.

I was going to leave the situation alone for now but best believe it was going to come back up at a later time. The rest of the ride Drix tried talking to me but I wasn't in the mood to hold a conversation with him. When we pulled up to Buffalo Wild Wings my foul mood was replaced by happiness, I love the Asian Zing wings they had.

"Eniko, come on. It's not even that serious you are getting mad for nothing," I heard as I stepped out the car. I looked around trying to figure out where the voice was coming from.

"Macy, it is that serious because I thought we were going out to eat alone. We have been with them for the majority of the week and I'm honestly tired of seeing Gavin's face."

My eyes landed the only two females I ever considered sisters. I walked right over to them as Drix called out my name. I was walking up behind Macy but if Eniko was paying any attention she would've seen me. I took Macy by her hair pulled her down then proceeded over to Eniko before she could realize what happened I slapped the shit out of her. I thought she was going to stand there and take that slap but she didn't. She leaned her hand back slapping me right back.

"Bitch!" Macy yelled, charging at me.

"Macy no!" Eniko called out.

"What you mean no you got to slap her back and know her ass deserves to hit the fucking ground."

"It's Emanii," Eniko told her. I was huffing and puffing while my chest heaved up and down.

"Yeah it's me and look who returned from the fucking dead," I sassed pissed the hell off.

They both looked at me for a second then reached out to give me a hug.

"Don't fucking touch me. The both of y'all just up and fucking disappeared like our friendship meant nothing. How could the two of y'all do that?" I was trying to come off tough but the hurt began to creep up in my voice.

"It's not what you think," Eniko sighed.

"We had no choice," Macy said.

"That doesn't explain to me how the two of you could just leave and not bother to even get in contact with me. You shutting out Haze was one thing Macy but the both of y'all shutting me out was fucking betrayal. And as soon as I drop this baby, I'm making it a point to run into the both of you and kick y'all asses."

"You're pregnant!" they said in unison.

"No bitches, I'm just fucking fat."

"Emanii, how the fuck you going to just walk away like I wasn't fucking calling yo ass?"

"Hey Drix," Eniko waved.

"Don't fucking say hi to my man. The only bitches his ass can be friendly too are my friends and the two of y'all ain't in that fucking category."

"Come on Manii. Let us explain!" Macy pleaded.

"I don't want to hear shit the two of you shady ass bitches got to say. Drix let's go," I told him.

"Manii, stop being emotional and hear them out. The three of y'all were close at one point and real friends are hard to find."

"Hendrix, I'm the one you have to come home to at night so are you sure you want to stick up for them?"

"Emanii, on some real shit since yo ass got pregnant you been thinkin' that you can talk to me any fuckin' way. I've been letting you get away with it cause you carrying my seed and shit but don't get it twisted, I will fuck yo little ass up. I'm not no bitch nigga so don't talk to me like one. Now go the fuck inside that restaurant with Macy and Eniko and let them explain what the fuck happened. Call me when you're done and I'll come pick you up." Drix kissed me on the cheek then left me standing there with these two bitches.

"Y'all heard my man let's go so y'all can explain to me what the fuck happened. Oh and y'all are buying my food too," I sassed then walked away in the direction of the restaurant.

The only reason I was going along with this is because Drix left me and he was my ride. I told the hostess we needed a table for three. We got seated right away and the awkwardness that filled the room had me feeling uneasy. I came off mad and angry towards them when in reality I was hurt. Macy and Eniko were the first real female friends I had and they just left me like it was nothing.

The waitress came over and took our order making this whole situation feel normal As soon as she left the awkward feeling came right back. I couldn't take it anymore and if we were going to fix this one of us had to start talking.

"This silence is awkward as hell so if one of you want to start explaining what happened then now would be the time."

"When everything happened with Liam as you know I was messed up behind it. I wasn't eating or anything like that. After I tried to jump in the casket my mother and Martin started talking about us moving away," Eniko explained.

"I heard the conversation, got mad, and ran to go see Haze. I went over there with the intensions on telling him what my father had planned but he hit me with his mother dying. There wasn't no way that I could tell him I was moving after he told me that his mother died. I spent some time with him before I went home. As soon as I stepped foot in the house my father took my phone away from me and snapped it in half. A couple of days later we were in a moving trucking moving to Philly."

"Okay but Eniko had her phone, she could've reached out."

"I actually left my phone in the old house. I wasn't in the right frame of mind so talking to anyone was the last thing on my mind. It may sound fucked up but it was the truth," Eniko told me.

"I don't have an excuse as to why I didn't reach out. I could've hit you up on Myspace or something but I honestly just didn't want to. I was going through heartbreak and you were linked to Haze, making me not want to be bothered with you. Not to mention I think it would be kind of wrong to reach out to you and talk to you but not talk to Haze. I was young back then and the only thing I was thinking bout was my heart being broken. I wasn't even really there for Eniko the way I should've been. I'm not trying to use that as an excuse or nothing, I'm just being honest. I will say that I am sorry for just leaving you in the dark like that," Macy apologized.

"I'm sorry too. We never meant to hurt you, Emanii. Like Macy said reaching out to you was too painful for us because you were connected to a lot of the pain that we were going through. I know that's not something you want to hear but it's the truth."

By the time they were done talking I was crying like a baby. Hearing them explain what happened did make me feel a little bit better about the situation, but I was still hurt. I was hurt because we had missed out on two years of each other's lives.

"Girl stop crying before someone think that you are going into labor." Macy joked.

"Shut up Macy," I laughed, trying to wipe the tears away. "Y'all just don't know how mad and hurt I've been behind the two of you leaving. We missed out on going to prom together and all that other stuff."

"We might have missed out on a lot but we have a second chance to build even more memories," Eniko smiled.

"What you mean? Wait, why are the two of you even in New York?"

"We are moving back!" they cheered.

"Really?"

"What you say it like that? You don't want us back?" Macy questioned.

"No it's not that I don't want y'all back, I just didn't think the two of you would ever move back here," I lied. The really reason I said really the way I did was because I knew it was going to be some shit. Them moving back meant that there was going to be a lot of uncertainty between them and Zeke and Haze.

"We actually moved back earlier this week. We are staying at Eniko's old house."

"I guess I can't believe that your parents let y'all come back."

"I couldn't believe it either but they want us to be adults." Eniko said. "Enough what's been up with you besides you getting pregnant."

"Honestly me getting pregnant is the biggest thing that has happened to me since the two of you left. After the two of y'all left I stayed to myself and just focused on school. The only time I went out was when I was with Zeke, Haze, and Drix."

"Don't make me feel bad." Macy sighed.

"No I guess it's a good thing that the two of you left because I threw myself into my books and graduated at the top of my class. I got a full ride to Columbia University."

"Oh shit you got in to Ivy League. Congratulations."

"Thank you Eniko, but I don't know if I'm gonna be able to go. I will be having the baby around the time school first starts."

"Okay what's the problem?"

"I don't know if I'm going to be able to handle a baby and being a full time student. I'm more so leaning towards community college for a year," I told them. I really wanted to go to Columbia I just didn't see how it was possible.

"You better not settle for a community college if you want to go to Columbia then that's what you do. It may be hard and tiring at times, but you just have to push through and stay focused on the big picture," Eniko encouraged.

"Yeah maybe." I sighed.

Going to Columbia was a conversation that I needed to have with Drix. I just haven't gotten around to it. I figured if I didn't have the conversation with him it would still be possible that I could go. I knew as soon as the conversation came up it would be put to rest. Drix was in the streets damn near all day so he wasn't going to baby sit for me. My mother was an option, but I didn't trust her completely to watch my child. Something was gonna have to give and nine times out of ten it would be me giving up Columbia.

"Rex just sent me a text saying him and Gavin are walking in now," Macy told Eniko.

"Why would you let them come in here when we are trying to catch up with Emanii," Eniko said in a harsh tone.

"He's just now texting me, what do you want me to do he is already here."

"Who are Rex and Gavin?" I questioned even though I already had a slight idea of who they were.

"Rex is her boyfriend and Gavin is his friend," Eniko told me.

"Oh, then I don't mind them being here."

The only reason I agreed to let the guys sit with us was because I wanted to size this Gavin dude up. Yeah Eniko claimed that he was just a friend of Rex but something else had to be going on because she instantly got annoyed as soon as Macy said his name. I wanted to at least let Zeke know what he was up against if he chose to try and win over Eniko.

"See, Manii doesn't mind them being here so why do you?"

"It's not that I mind them being here I just don't want to deal with Gavin."

They continued to go back and forth never noticing the two guys coming straight for our table. When they reached our table I gave them both the once over and was pleased with what I saw. Rex was cute but he didn't have anything on Gavin. Gavin was fine with a capital F, he had to come with nothing but issues because I didn't see any other reason for Eniko to turn his ass down.

"Emanii, this is my boyfriend Rex and his friend Gavin. Rex and Gavin, this is our best friend Emanii."

"I wouldn't say that I'm their best friend, but we cool. It's nice to meet you." I smiled.

"Wassup," Rex and Gavin said, giving me a head nod.

Rex sat next to Macy on the opposite of Eniko and I while Gavin sat at the end of the table. The waitress came back over with our drinks then took our food order, once she left I decided to be nosy a little bit.

"So Gavin and Rex how old are y'all?"

"Rex is twenty and I'm twenty-one," Gavin answered.

"What about you?" Rex asked.

"Oh I turned eighteen on the Fourth of July."

"That's next week, happy early birthday, ma," Rex said.

"What are you doing for your birthday?" Eniko asked.

"I don't know it's not like I can do much. I may just have a cookout at the house or something."

"Whatever you decide to do make sure that Eniko and I are invited.

"I'll think about it." I joked. "What do the two of you do?" I was making sure I asked all the appropriate questions so if things popped off between my brother and them he would know how to solve the problem.

"What I do remains my business and no one else's, feel me?" When Rex said that I already knew he was in the streets.

"Nigga, chill the fuck out. She not the feds or no shit man." Gavin laughed.

"No it's cool I understand, I'm not offended."

"It's not about you being offended it's about this nigga always trying to bring the street code into every situation," Gavin explained.

"If you live the street code twenty-four seven then it's only right that he brings it everywhere he goes. He got to make sure that the two of you don't get caught up," I told him.

"I feel you on that but when you not in the street life it gets tiring when you have to hear the g code every day."

"Nigga, stop acting like you weren't part of that life," Rex told him.

"Yeah I was and I'll never deny that shit. But I'm not in that shit no more."

"If you don't mind me asking what made you get out the game? I mean you're only twenty-one which means you weren't in the game for long," I asked him. I was probably over stepping my boundaries and I didn't care. He wanted to put it out there leaving me no other option than to dig for more information.

"The shit wasn't for me. It doesn't take years to figure out what was for you and what wasn't. I just graduated from Penn with my Bachelor's in accounting. In my sophomore year of college, I realized that hustling was more so Rex's thing. I wasn't going to leave my boy hanging though, so now I just handle all his money and shit."

"Excuse me," Eniko said damn near pushing me out of the booth.

"Hold on Eniko, damn. Where are you going?"

"I need to go to the bathroom," she told me.

"Okay I'll come with you because this baby is playing soccer with my bladder."

We went to the bath and as soon as we got in there Eniko started talking a mile a minute.

"Oh my god, he doesn't sell drugs. I'm so stupid this whole time he was trying to get with me I played him to the left because I assumed he sold drugs because Rex did. That's probably why he was shaking his head at me the other day."

"Eniko, what are you talking about?" I went into the bathroom stall waiting for her to answer because I couldn't hold my pee anymore.

"Gavin he has been trying to get with me since I met him. I refused to go on a date with him because I thought he sold drugs."

I came out the stall and went straight for the sink. "Well now that you know he doesn't sell drugs what are you going to do?"

"I'm going to go on a date with his ass. I know you seen how fine he is." She smiled.

"Yeah he is cute but just because he doesn't sell drugs doesn't mean you should jump at the chance to date him."

"What do you mean?"

"He may not sell drugs but he handles Rex's money which mean that nigga ain't too legal. It might look good that he got a degree from an Ivy League but his hands are still dirty." I wasn't telling her this to sway her decision I was telling her because it was the truth. It didn't matter if your hands were touching actually drugs or not. When it came down to an indictment or something everyone involved was getting charged. This was one of the main reasons why I wanted to study law. If something was to happen to Zeke, Haze, and Drix, I could be the one to help get them out of their situation.

"That's true," Eniko agreed.

"I'm just saying that's something to think about." I shrugged.

We exited out of the bathroom and went back to the table. The rest of our lunch went by smoothly. Leaving out I honestly didn't know how to feel about Macy and Eniko. I mean I still loved them as sisters, but I still felt the pain of them leaving for two years. They were only in Philly so I didn't understand the complete cut off of communication. Maybe it was because New York reminded them of so much hurt and I was linked to the hurt, they weren't the only ones that were hurt in the situation though. Liam may not have been my boyfriend but he was someone that I grew up with so the same pain Eniko felt I felt.

Even though I was still in my feelings about the whole situation I wasn't going to hold it against them. Macy and Eniko both seemed like they wanted to repair our friendship and I was all for that. It wasn't going to go back to how it used to be overnight, but I was willing to get it there if they were.

## 6: Zeke

"I called this meeting to make sure that everyone in this room is on the same page as the person standing to the left of them. We came along way from the corners and I refuse to go back." I paused to skim the room and make sure that everyone was paying attention.

"For the past five months Trey you have been bringing in fifty thousand at the end of the month, right?" I asked.

"Yeah that's right," he said.

"Then why the fuck is the bag that Haze picked up last night five dollars short?"

"Man, I don't know but I know that shit don't got shit to do with me," he told me.

"So you mean to tell me that my cousin is stealing from himself?" Haze was standing on the right of me and Drix was to my left. They both smirked while their low chuckles could be heard throughout the room.

"I mean if that's what you want to chalk it up to be. I can't tell you where those five dollars went. No one at my spot is pressed for five dollars," he explained.

"Haze, you pressed for five dollars my nigga?"

"Why the fuck would I be pressed for five dollars for when I got more than a stack in my pocket." Haze pulled out two knots and placed them on the coffee table that sat in front of us.

"So as you can see Trey, my niggas not pressed for money and I understand that you not pressed for money, but we have an issue that needs a resolution."

"You want me to give you the five dollars or some shit," he gritted, going in his pocket and peeling off a five-dollar bill from his wallet.

"Trey, you not understanding where I'm coming from my g. You run that spot that came up five dollars short. So that means you have to deal with the consequences and unfortunately you just can't give me five dollars and think everything is going to be cool."

"Then what you want Zeke damn, I told you I would give you the money back."

"Nigga, I want your fucking life."

As if it was nothing Haze, Drix and I each put a single bullet into Trey's head. It exploded causing his brain, skull, and blood to splatter everywhere. I watched to see if anyone was going to jump back from the shit. Everyone remained in their seats without even flinching.

"When it comes to my fucking money and product I don't play about that shit. Come correct or sign your death certificate. Ryan, with Trey dead his spot is now yours. Make sure you don't fuck up the same way he did, ight."

"I got you," Ryan answered.

"Clean this shit up and get ready to get back to work tomorrow at six in the morning!" Drix ordered.

Haze, Drix, and I left out of the apartment and headed for our cars in the parking lot.

"It's a good thing we keep silencers on our shit whenever we have a meeting, cause if not we would be all fucked up with the way this nigga be ready kill the whole team," Haze said.

"You can't talk cause you ain't no better, my nigga." Drix clowned him.

We used the apartment that we first started working out of for our meetings because the shit was just more convenient.

"Nah, that nigga killed ole boy for five dollars. He would've at least had to be ten dollars short for me to kill him." Haze laughed.

"That nigga's hands are the last ones that touch the money before it gets to us. If his needy ass can steal five fucking dollars then who knows what the fuck else he is willing to steal. Never allow something so small get passed you because once niggas think you not paying attention they and pull the wool over your eyes leaving you to kill more niggas on your team than you have to," I told them.

Being in this game for the last three years has taught me some things. I always made sure I observed every and anything before acting. Wasn't no nigga gonna ever catch me on some late or premature shit. I

"I hear you my nigga but cut that knowledge dropping shit. That's more so Drix's flow," Haze told me.

"Ain't no knowledge dropping. I'm speaking nothing but the truth."

"Yeah, yeah nigga," Haze waved me off laughing.

"Man, tell me why when I went to take Emanii to Buffalo Wild Wings, her ass tried to fight Macy and Eniko."

"Hol' up they were there?" I questioned.

"Yeah man. Emanii flipped out on they ass," Drix said, shaking his head.

"Where Manii at now? Is she cool?"

"Yeah she good I left her there with they ass."

"Drix, the fuck would you do that for? Manii don't need to be around Macy's trifling ass," Haze gritted.

"Just cause you got your issues with Macy doesn't mean Emanii has to have them issues too. She hurting behind what they did and the only way to fix the pain is to face that shit head on," Drix told him.

"Fuck that shit I don't want my cousin around them bitches."

"Haze, Drix's got a point. You can't expect Emanii to borrow your beef bruh," I told him.

"She's my family which means family rides together. Macy ain't got no heart anyone so that friendship ain't going to do shit but fail just like the first time. I'm up out of here though." Haze dapped us up then jumped in his car and peeled off.

"That nigga's bugging."

"He may not want to say the shit out loud but Macy broke his heart," I told Drix.

"Yeah I know. I still think he taking the shit too far. I'm about to go and pick up Manii now," he said, looking at his phone.

"I'ma follow you over there so I can pick up some wings."

"What you want I'll tell Manii to ordered it so it will be ready when you get there."

"I want a twenty piece Thai Curry," I told him

"Ight."

I got in my car with only one thing on my mind and it damn sure wasn't those wings.

*  *  *

I stepping out the car I went over to where Drix was waiting for me against his car.

"They should be coming out soon," he told me.

I nodded my head but didn't say anything. On the outside I was calm, cool, and collected but on the inside I was trying to figure what to say to Eniko. I could've spit game at her but she wasn't even the type of chick that would go for something like that. There wasn't even a point in me spitting game because it wasn't like I was trying to get to know her, I already knew her. I just needed her to talk to me. I just wanted to have a conversation with her.

"Here they come now."

I looked towards the entrance of the sports bar and saw Emanii, Macy and Eniko walk out along with two dudes. My jaw instantly started flexin' before I even knew who the two dudes were. I kept my eyes on Eniko as Manii said a couple of things to her and Macy. Manii must've told them that I was over there with Drix because they both looked in my direction. Macy said something to the two dudes then all three of them walked towards Drix and I. The two dudes stared at the girls until they made it over to us then walked off.

"Why the two of you leaning up against the car like y'all hot shit?" Manii joked.

"I don't know about Drix but I'm the hottest thing on the block. Wassup Macy?"

"Hey Zeke." She leaned over giving me a hug while Eniko stood there trying to look at everything but me.

"Wassup Eniko, you can't speak or something," I said, messing with her.

"Hi Zeke."

"Damn what I do to you? That greeting was flat as hell."

"What else did you expect for me to say Zeke?" she questioned.

"Nothing. Take a ride with me."

"No I'm cool. Macy and I have to get going."

"For what? We don't have anything to do but unpack the rest of the stuff."

"Y'all moved back to the city?"

"Yea Zeke we did," Eniko sassed, rolling her eyes.

"That's wassup. I won't hold you tho. Macy it's was good seeing you."

"You too Zeke. Drix congrats on the baby and Emanii I will call you later."

"Congrats Drix and I'll be on the phone call too," Eniko chimed in.

"Thank y'all."

The both walked off and I couldn't help but to stare at Eniko as she walked away. She standing here she was beautiful but when she walked away she became delicious.

"How you just going to let her walk away like that?" Emanii asked, punching me in the arm.

"Keep yo hands to yo self. I don't mind flicking you in the forehead until you drop that load and then I can fuck you up for real," I told her.

"Nigga, did you just say flick?" Drix questioned with laughter in his voice.

"Hell yeah I did. She's over here hitting on me like I don't got a plan. You back cool with them?"

"I wouldn't say we are back cool, but we are cordial," she answered.

"Cordial enough to invite them to your birthday party?"

"Yeah."

"Ight, thanks sis I love you." I kissed her on the forehead then headed for my car.

"I love you too. Don't wait too long because she's feeling one of the dudes that we had lunch with."

"Who's the other dude?" Drix asked her.

"Macy's boyfriend."

"That's that nigga from the joint out in Philly. Haze got a death wish for that nigga."

"Yeah that other nigga got one too. Be safe ight," I told them then headed for my car.

Eniko could think her little attitude was gonna push me away but she had another thing coming. As far as her and dude that was a dead situation. I wasn't on some if I can't have you then no one else can have you type shit, but I wasn't going to allow her to fuck with anyone else. I did that once and I wasn't going to make the same mistake twice. With Lemon out of the way I had all the room I needed to make my move on her.

## 7: *Haze*

"You sure you want me to leave? Last night was so fun we can just do it all over again." Gigi said as she slowly slid her panties up her legs.

"That's what I told you I wanted, right?"

Licking my lips, I stared at the sight in front of me. Gigi had on nothing besides the panties she just put on. The morning sun danced against her chocolate skin, causing her to look like a snack. I know I told her to leave but looking at her right now had me rethinking that decision.

"Those words might have escaped your mouth, that doesn't mean that's really what you want," she purred. "I'm gonna go to the bathroom and when I come back if you still want me to leave then you got it."

I smirked at her because Gigi was like no other. When you tell most woman the only thing you got for them is dick they run or they try to change your ways. Gigi accepted the shit, she told me pussy and soft skin was the only she had to offer me and I was cool with that. I met Gigi a month ago at Webster Hall. She seemed cool so I grabbed her number just to see what was up with her. The first night I took her out she told me she wasn't looking for a relationship. She had just got out of a four-year relationship that she had been in since high school and she wanted to have some fun. I damn sure wasn't looking for a relationship so shit worked out perfectly for the two of us.

After leaving Zeke and Drix last night I came straight to the crib and called her up. Hearing Macy's name had me on ten and I need a relief. At some point I was gonna have to face her because we were bound to run into each other with her hanging back out with Emanii. When the time came I would face but for right now I didn't want to hear shit about her ass. Call me salty, I didn't give a fuck.

"So did you change your mind or am I still leaving." Gigi was standing in the door of my bedroom with one hand playing in her hair and the other one sliding down her stomach.

"I wish I could dive back in that chocolate thang you got between your legs, but I got moves that need to be made."

"Fine, if that's what you want."

While she came in the room to get dressed, I went in the bathroom to handle my hygiene. I made sure to grab my phone on the way out to check if I had any missed calls or text messages. Scrolling through my phone, I had a couple of missed calls from chicks I used to fuck but nothing major.

Thirty minutes later I was fresh out the shower and ready to get dressed and make some moves. Going back into the room Gigi was no longer there, as she has done many times before there was note that said until next time on my dresser. Going in my closet I pulled out a pair of truey jeans and a plain black t-shirt. I had money but dressing over the top wasn't my style. On occasion I could be flashy but most of the time I kept it simple. I pulled my Space Jams from out the closet and threw them on then headed out the door.

Jumping in my car I headed over to a couple of our sports to make sure shit was straight what happened yesterday with Trey. I didn't even feel bad for Trey cause that nigga should've known better. Young Savages might have played about a lot of shit but none of us played when it came to money. That nigga could've been a penny off and he still would've ended up dying. Playing with a man's money is similar to playing with their livelihood and none of us was having that. Hearing Jay Z rapping the about pledging your allegiance to Roc Nation had me pulling my phone out my pocket. Emanii was calling so I picked it up without thinking twice.

"Yo!"

"Why must you be so niggerish Haze? I know Auntie raised you better than that. I'm not one of your friends in the street; greet me with a hello when you answer the phone."

Love & The Come 2

"I didn't know it was you my bad," I lied

"Stop lying, you don't answer the phone without looking at the caller ID."

"Ight you got me, damn. What you want big head?"

"It's not so much of what I want it's more so what your aunt wants. You know when Auntie died my mom never got to say good bye because she was dealing with her own demons. Well I'm sitting with her now and she wants to know if you can take her to go see her sister."

"Manii, you know I don't like going to my mom's burial site. Why can't you take her?"

"I know Haze and I tried to get her to let me take her but she wants you to take her. If you can't then it's cool I'll just drag her ass there or she just won't go."

"Give me until later and I'll let you know something."

"Okay Haze," she said "You still coming to family dinner tonight, right?"

"You already that is a must," I told her then hung up the phone.

Instead of going right into the spot I sat outside for a minute. I haven't been to my mother's burial site since I laid her to rest. Going back there was just too painful and brought back memories I wasn't too fond of. I loved my aunt to death and I would do anything for her, this one thing though I wasn't going to be able to do. I lost my mother and girl in the same day and that caused a pain I wasn't sure too many people could understand. Sadness washed over me just thinking about it. I sent Emanii a text letting her know that I wasn't gonna be able to make that trip. She hit me right back with the sad faces but said she understood.

Pulling myself together I tucked my phone in my back pocket then headed into the spot. Sooner or later I was gonna have to go back to my mother gravesite and deal with my issues but that shit wasn't going to be today.

* * *

"Damn Manii, you not going to say nothing your favorite cousin?" I asked, walking in the house. Once a month we had a family dinner and since Drix was the only one out of us who had a girl, it was always held at his house.

"You aren't my favorite cousin right now, because of you I had to hear my mother complain for two hours about not being able to go to the gravesite."

"I told you I wasn't going to be able to take her and you said you understood."

"Yeah I do understand but that doesn't mean I wanted to hear my mother complain."

"I don't see why she just wouldn't let you take her."

"You still haven't been to Auntie's gravesite since we buried her? Zeke asked me.

"Nah." I shook my head.

"I don't blame him I know that shit can't be easy," Drix said.

"That shit ain't easy bring back too many emotions that I'm not trying to deal with right now."

"I hear that shit because emotions will get your ass caught up," Drix agreed.

"What did you just say?" Emanii asked him.

"I said emotions will get your ass caught up and you know that shit is true. You got caught up yesterday behind them shits."

"When I saw Eniko and Macy yesterday I did not get caught up in my emotions. They deserved what they got because what they did was foul but I'm passed that now."

"Why y'all always trying to bring up Macy's name and shit now?"

"Haze stop acting like that you're gonna have to talk to her at some point."

"I don't have to talk to her ever. Just cause you made up with shawty doesn't mean I have to."

"Well she's going to be at my party next week so you can talk to her then and get all this anger out that you have towards her."

"The fuck you invite her to the party for? Y'all haven't even been back cool for that long and you want to invite her to family functions and shit."

"Haze it's really not that serious," Zeke said.

"It might not be serious to y'all and that's cool because I don't expect y'all to understand. I'm up out of here though," I told them.

"Haze don't leave, you didn't even eat yet!" Emanii pleaded.

"Yeah chill out bruh stop getting all emotional on us," Zeke said.

"Nah, I'm good."

I bypassed all of them and headed for the door. A nigga wasn't even pissed, I was more so upset about the whole Macy shit. For the past two years I masked all the hurt I was feeling about Macy leaving with anger. I was wildin' out in these streets just to not think about her or the bullshit she did. With her being back and these niggas constantly talking about her my true feelings were starting to show. I wasn't ready to deal with the Macy shit and I honestly thought I wouldn't be seeing her ass for a minute. But fuck it since she was going to be at Macy's birthday party I had no choice other than to face her and I knew for a fact that shit wasn't going to end pretty.

## 8: Eniko

"You gonna let me take you out or are we going to continue to have these late night phone calls?" Gavin's deep raspy voice was music to my ears. Whenever he talked to me I would instantly feel like I could drift off to sleep.

"I have a birthday party to go to."

"I don't want to hear that shit. You been duckin' going out with me since I met you. You said it was because I was in the streets but I don't live that life, ma. Now you making excuses and shit cause you gotta go to a birthday party."

"I'm not making excuses."

"Then what the hell you doing, Eniko? It's either you going to go out with me or I'ma kidnap yo ass. Either one works good for me, how about you?"

"Really Gavin you would kidnap me just to get me to go on a date with you?" I played like I was annoyed by what he said when in reality I was flattered. It's been almost a week since we went to Buffalo Wild Wings and Gavin and I talk on the phone every night since. I was still holdin' off going on a date with him because he may not have been in the streets but he was still cleaning up dirty money.

"Eniko, you think I'm playing when I'm being so dead ass. I want you and anything I want I get even if I have to take it. So the question is are you going to make me take or are you gonna come on your own." My legs silently trembled when he asked me was he gonna have to take it. My body was ready for Gavin but my heart and mind frame wasn't. I was over the situation that happened with Liam but the pain was still there.

"Matter of fact I ain't even going to give you a chance to make a decision. I'll be at your house by eight tomorrow. That's more than enough time for you to be at that party. If you ain't home by the time I get there then I'm just gonna step back. I leave to go back to Philly this Sunday so it's either we going to do this or we not. You may not want to say it but you are making me pay for someone else's mistakes and that shit ain't fair. It ain't fair to me and it damn sure not fair to yourself. I'll hit you tomorrow around eight, ma." He didn't even let me say anything he just hung up the phone.

I went to dial him back but when I did the phone went straight to voicemail. I sent his ass a text letting him know I didn't appreciate being sent to voicemail. I threw my phone on the bed and fell back throwing a pillow over my face so I could yell into it. I was so frustrated that it didn't make any sense.

"What's wrong with you?" Macy asked, barging into my room.

"Nothing." I usually talked to Macy about any and everything but this right here wasn't something I was sure she could relate too. In the past Macy had tried to push me into talking to boys and when I told her why I didn't want to she would just tell me that the past was in the past and I needed to move on. That was easy for her to say because Haze was still alive while Liam rotted in the ground. She just seemed so unapologetic and harsh whenever it came to guy talk.

"I know you're lying and I'm not going to push you to talk, but I have something I need to tell you." She sighed.

"What?"

Macy walked over to my bed and sat Indian style at the end of it. She picked up a pillow and laid it across her lap.

"I'm scared to go to the Emanii's birthday cookout tomorrow."

"Why?"

"I'm more than certain Haze is going to be there. The last time I saw him the nigga had a gun to my head. I can only imagine what he's going to do when he sees me this time."

"I mean at some point the two of you are gonna have to have a conversation about what happened back then. I think you owe him an explanation and he owes you an apology."

*Love & The Come 2*

"I just rather not do it at the birthday party you know. When I saw him in Philly I promise you my heart wanted to jump out of my chest and into his hands. Seeing him did something to me that I can't even describe."

"You still have feelings for him? Do you still love him?"

"I will probably always love Haze, he was my first love and yeah the feelings are still there. I've always said that if I didn't move away Haze and I would still be together."

"But y'all aren't together and you have a whole boyfriend."

"I know I have a boyfriend and I care about Rex, but I don't love him."

"Then why are you still with him if you don't love him?" I always knew that Macy didn't love Rex you could just see it when you looked at the two of them. They were a cute couple but one was more into the other person.

"He makes me happy you know. He is the only dude that hasn't really pushed me into saying things that I'm not ready to say. It's not like he doesn't know that I don't love him. We had that conversation before. He knows I care about him and he also knows that something I went through is stopping me from saying those words to him. He's cool with

*103*

the way our relationship is and so am I. Why mess up a good thing, right?"

"Why keep something that's not a good thing? You stay with Rex and someone is going to get hurt. Just from talking to you I can read between everything that you are saying."

"Then what am I saying since you know so much, Eniko," she sassed along with a roll of her eyes.

"Just let me ask you a question. If Haze was to say let's give us another try would you tell him yes or would you tell him you had a boyfriend?"

"Eniko, that's not fair."

"It's a fair question because there might be a possibility that it might happen."

"Then I'll cross that bridge when I get there. Right now I just need to prepare myself for when I see him. How did you handle seeing Zeke?"

"What do you mean how did I handle seeing Zeke? I never had any ties to him besides the feelings I had for him before Liam and I got together."

"Yeah but I saw the way you were looking at him when we were talking to him outside of Buffalo Wild Wings. The feelings you had for him were present in that moment and so were his for you."

"Macy, you're putting too much on that. Was I nervous when I say him, yes. Did I feel a little something when I saw him, yeah but none of that means anything because he was Liam's best friend. I'm not about to be loving the crew."

Even if Zeke wasn't Liam's best I still wouldn't fuck with his ass. Those two years did him good and he was looking finer than ever but one thing remained the same, he was still the streets and I wasn't having that.

"So does that mean you are going to give Gavin a chance?" The goofy smile she had on her face caused me to laugh because she was so stupid.

"I don't know he asked me on a date then hung up on me when I told him I had a birthday party to go to."

"If I was Gavin I would've stopped trying to mess with you a long time ago."

"I'm worth the fight I guess."

"He's not in the streets so what's stopping you from dating him now. Gavin is beyond cute and he got some good hair. You better jump on that before someone else does."

"He lives all the way in Philly how are we supposed to make a relationship work?"

"Stop with the excuses because you know Philly is just a hop and a skip away. What's really stopping you from giving him a chance."

"It's just…" I paused for a second then continued. "Liam was the first boy I ever loved, I gave him a special piece of me and the next thing I know he died. That created a pain that only someone who been through that experience will understand. I'm nervous about even dating anyone else because I don't ever want to experience that pain again. I wouldn't say that I'm a virgin but I'm close as hell to being one and what if I give Gavin my body and he just walks out on me or dies. I don't think I would be able to go through that whole thing a second time. The first time it nearly broke me I'm for certain getting hurt like that again would kill me."

"I'm not going to sit here and say that I understand what you're saying because I honestly don't. I don't even know if I have the right words to say to try and make you feel better. What I can say is that not everything is going to bring you pain. For all you know Gavin might be the perfect guy for you and then on the other hand he might just be the perfect mistake you ever made. Either way you are never going to know by just shutting him down. I'm not going to lie to you and tell you that hurt and pain doesn't come with relationships because they do. We aren't fourteen turning fifteen anymore Eniko, how simple a relationship was back then isn't going to be how simple a relationship is now. The hurt and the pain that you are afraid of experiencing again will never kill you because you are a lot stronger then you give yourself credit for.

You stayed strong while you were going through the emotions of Liam's death. I on the other hand went and dated boys trying to fill the whole where my heart was supposed to be all because I didn't want to feel the pain. You faced your pain head on and that makes you stronger than you would ever know."

"I don't know if I can be strong twice Macy. I just don't know if I can go through being hurt again!" By now, I was crying because this was something that I knew I had to deal with if I was ever going to be with someone.

"Stop thinking about the worse that can happen and think about all the great things that can come from you being in a relationship. The more you think about the bad things the more you are psyching yourself out and the only thing that is going to do is cause you to inflict hurt and pain on yourself because you will be missing out on so much. You are eighteen Eniko, dating and figuring things out is what we are supposed to be doing right now. Nothing is going to be perfect and we don't need it to be. As long as I am breathing, you will always have me when things don't seem to go the way you would like them to. We are sisters and I promise that I'm going to be here going through whatever with you. We're a team forever baby."

I looked at Macy and couldn't help but to smile. Everything she was saying to me was right. I couldn't let the past hurt and pain stop me from exploring certain things. If I were to endure anymore hurt and pain then I would just do my best to get passed it the same way I did with Liam's death.

"I'ma go on the date," I told her.

"Aye, that's my girl. Just make sure you don't have sex. Sex on the first date is a no-no," she joked.

"You don't have to worry about that. He's in timeout for hanging up the phone on me."

"I hear that. Let's order some pizza or something I'm hungry as hell."

"Order me bacon and pepperoni on my side," I told her, picking up my phone.

I scrolled to Gavin's name and sent him a text saying that I would be ready for our date tomorrow and for him not to be late. After sending the message butterflies filled my stomach as I waited to see if he was going to respond. Not even a minute later I was receiving a text from him.

**Gavin:** *I see u got some act right. That's wassup ma. I'll be there at eight tomorrow night.*

Seeing the text caused my heart rate to slow down some and I felt a lot better about the situation. I wasn't going to go into this situation with any negative thoughts or positive ones. I was just going to let whatever happens happen. I was going to prepare myself to deal with the good, bad, and ugly that may come my way because I couldn't just keep shutting people out because I was scared of the hurt and pain that may come with them. As Macy said, I was eighteen and wasn't nothing going to be perfect for me right now. Gavin could either be perfect for me or a perfect mistake, either way I could say at least I gave him a chance.

## 9: Macy

*Come on Macy stop acting like you a punk bitch. You're Macy Renee Taylor! You not scared of anyone. Seeing Haze isn't going to be nothing but a walk in the park. You over here trippin' about seeing Haze when he's not even the reason you came over here. You came here to celebrate Emanii's birthday. If things go south with Haze just ignore his goofy looking ass. Yeah that's exactly what you do ignore his ass.*

As Eniko and I made our way toward Emanii's backyard, I gave myself a pep talk. My stomach was bubbling and my hands were sweating. Just the possibility of me seeing Haze had me acting out of character and I didn't like it at all. No matter how many times I tried to tell myself that seeing Haze wasn't a big deal I knew I was lying to myself. The closer we got to the gate the bigger my panic attack became. My sweaty hands began to shake as I tried to steady them and bounce back. This shit was crazy because I haven't seen dude in two years and he was doing something to me that was so unexplainable and his ass wasn't nowhere in sight.

"Are you okay?" Eniko stopped in front of the gate looking at me strangely.

"Eniko I don't think I can do this. My heart is racing and my hands are sweaty. My ass is over here looking like I'm on drugs or something. I can't go in there looking like this." I turned around ready to take my ass back to the car. Eniko grabbed my hand and pulled me back towards the gate.

"Eniko, let me go so I can leave. I'll sit in the car until you're ready to go if I have to."

"Macy, pull yourself together because you're not about to leave me here alone. The same way you told me you we—e going to be there for me last night is the same way I'm about to be here for you now. All this shaking and sweating you're doing it's because you're putting too much on this. Haze isn't a big deal, trust me you are just making him into one. Breath and relax. Stay with me for a couple of hours and if you still want to leave then we can go alright?"

"I don't know Enik—"

"I don't want to hear that you don't know nothing. You are about to go in here and act like Haze doesn't even exist."

"Fine Eniko."

She took my hand in hers then pushed the gate open. We barely had two feet in the backyard when the music suddenly stopped and all eyes fell on us. I wasn't sure if this was a coincidence or a set up. Either way the attention that I was receiving was something I could've down without.

"Stop staring like you never seen two beautiful girls before," I heard Emanii say. It took her a minute to get through the crowd of people but when she did she pulled us both into a hug.

"I'm so happy the two of you came." She smiled.

"You know we wouldn't miss your birthday boo," Eniko told her.

"I mean the two of you did miss about three of my birthdays. But I'm hoping that the gift bag I see in y'all hands are gifts that make up for those missed birthdays." She smiled.

"How did I know you were going to say something slick like that," I laughed, rolling my eyes playfully at her.

"No seriously come with me and we can put them gifts in the house and then get some food."

We followed her inside and the whole way I kept looking around waiting for my eyes to connect with his. Our eyes never connected and the breath I didn't know I was holding escaped my mouth followed by a sigh.

"You can stop looking for him because he's not here yet," Emanii told me while taking our gift bags out of our hands.

"What? I'm not looking for nobody," I lied, trying to play it cool.

"Stop. If we are going to make this friendship work again then we need to be honest with each other."

"She has a point," Eniko agreed.

"Fine. I'm nervous as hell about running into Haze because the last time we ran into each other it wasn't too pretty. I'm not trying to mess up your birthday or anything so the quicker I see him the quicker whatever is going to happen can happen.

"How do you even know something is going to happen? The more you think something negative is going to happen the more you are speaking it into existence. I know Haze and trust me he wouldn't show his ass at my birthday party. So you have nothing to worry about," Emanii informed me.

"And even if he did show his ass you have me there to beat his ass."

"Eniko is right as long as I'm around I refuse to let Haze disrespect you."

"Awwww I love you guys!" I cried lightly pulling them into a group hug.

With Emanii back in the circle I felt like things were whole again. With it just being Eniko and I our issues were kind of becoming too much. It was like we were always going through something at the same time. Emanii was going to be the balance between us because neither one of us would have to only depend on one person's opinion. To sum it all up I was happy as hell that I had my girl back.

"Enough of all this sentimental shit. I may not be able to drop it like it's hot anymore but I expect my two bitches to make it do what it do." Emanii smiled.

The three of us headed out of the house and into the backyard where everyone was having fun. The DJ was playing all the hits and we were having a ball dancing. We spent the next four hours dancing, eating, reminiscing and laughing. I was really enjoying myself and any thoughts of Haze were long gone. He hadn't shown his face yet and I was perfectly fine with that. The day started to turn to night as and it was time for Emanii to cut her cake. Everyone crowded around her as Drix stood to her left, Zeke stood to her right and Eniko and I were standing next to Haze.

"I know y'all weren't going to cut the cake without me. Manii, how you gonna do your favorite cousin like that."

My body became stiff instantly from hearing his voice. As if the world was drawing us to each other our eyes connected. I wanted to look away so badly but our gaze was set in stone and there was no breaking it. I swallowed hard not knowing exactly what was going to happen next.

"Haze! You know I was going to save you the biggest piece!" Emanii screamed. She moved by her cake and rushed over to him giving him a hug. "I wasn't sure you were going to make it."

"Wasn't nothing going to stop me from being here for you, Manii. It's your day ma nothing else matters." The look he gave when he said nothing else mattered crushed my heart. It was if he was talking those words directly to my soul and they cut deep.

He gave Emanii a kiss on the forehead then let her go. She took her place back in front of her cake and the singing started all over. Haze found his way standing directly behind me. He was so close to me that if I bent over to pick something up my ass would rub against his front of his pants. In the middle of everyone singing happy birthday to Emanii, Haze slipped his fingers into my belt loops and forcefully pulled me into his chest. I wasn't that far away from him so the impact from me hitting his chest caused us to stumble back some. I continued singing trying my hardest not to let him have an effect on me. He nestled his face into the crook of my neck and the feeling of his cool breath on my skin sent a chill down my body and a tingle sensation between my legs. Any singing that I was doing before stopped the moment he started whispering sweet nothings in to my ear.

"I miss you, ma. You fucked my head up when you left me."

His husky voice turnt me on even more. I didn't know what to say or do in this moment. I was afraid that if I said or did the wrong thing this beautiful moment would be ruined. It was less than a month ago that he held a gun to my head and now he wanted to be all up on me. As far as what I should say I was confused, the feelings I was experiencing right now weren't confusing at all. While he was holding me I couldn't but to think about all the good times we had which caused old feeling to arise. My body melted into his as we stood there body to body. Right now there wasn't anywhere I wanted to be other than in his arms.

"Uh Macy, are you going to get some cake before we leave because I'm ready to go. I have to go home and get ready for my date," Eniko said, interrupting the moment Haze and I was sharing.

"You leaving already, ma? Eniko, you can't speak or nothing? You just going to stare at a nigga like he got two heads or some shit."

"I think I'm going to continue to stare at you like you got two heads because it's clear as day that you got more than one personality. How are you hugged up on her after you were ready to end her life?"

"Eniko!" I yelled.

"Nah it's cool, she's right. That's my bad," he said.

"That's all you have to say about the situation is that it's your bad? What if you would've shot her and killed her would it be your bad then too?"

"The fuck else you want me to say? I acted on my emotions. I'm over that shit and you need to be too."

"Like hell I am, what you did was fucked up and Macy deserves a better apology than my bad. Macy, are you seriously going to stay wrapped up in his arms?"

"Eniko, this isn't the place to have the conversation." I told her wishing she would shut the hell up.

"You don't think I know that Eniko? What the fuck Macy did was fucked up too but you don't see one of my boys dragging her behind that bullshit. If I can forgive her for that shit then she can forgive me for putting a gun in her face. You forgive me right, Macy?" He spun me around forcing me to look into his pretty ass eyes. Any common sense I had went out the window the moment his thick tongue slid across his thick lips.

"Yeah I forgive you, pa," I cooed. It was like I was in trance right now and I never wanted to be snapped out of it.

"Macy, let me talk to you for a minute over here." Eniko did very little to mask the distaste she had for Haze at the moment.

"Macy, catch up with me before you blow out of here." Haze leaned down kissing me oh so softly on my lips then walked away. I wanted to slap the shit out of Eniko for stepping into business that had nothing to do with her.

"What the hell are you buggin' for? I snapped. "You were supposed to snap if Haze showed his ass not if he is acting right." I walked away from her because Emanii was cutting her cake and I didn't want her guest all in my business more than they already were.

"What do you mean what am I buggin' for? He could've fuckin' killed out that day Macy. Does that even matter to you anymore? Or is the fact that he is all up on you clouding your better judgement.

"Why are you so concerned? I'm not buggin' about him shooting me and neither should you. This is my business not yours."

"I can't even believe that you are acting like this. It's crazy how him being all hugged up on you has got you acting like one of these bimbo chicks. Is him whispering in your ear and holding you close all it takes for you to forgive him?"

"He's not tripping about me leaving and I'm not tripping about him pointing a gun at me so just leave it alone. You're looking for me to have an attitude with him when there isn't a reason for me to have one. We both hurt each other but it's in the past know and that's exactly where I plan on leaving it. Don't you have a date or something to get ready for instead of worrying about me, damn."

Eniko was really blowing my high right now. I didn't want to argue with her or nothing. All I wanted was to live in the moment and she was killing the shit fast.

"Don't you have a boyfriend that you need to be worrying about instead of being hugged up with your ex.?" she snapped right back at me.

"Yeah, I do have a boyfriend and he's not here right now which makes him irrelevant at this moment. Haze has always been and held my heart in his hand. Just now proved that our love is stronger than anything that can try and pull us apart. If you want to call me crazy then I'll be that.

"What the hell did he do to you? He pointed a gun at you and you're just going to forgive him instantly." Disappointment dripped from her words as she talked to me.

"He didn't do nothing but remind me of something I already knew. You told me earlier that you would be here for me and support me. Well where is the support now? If you wanted to be with Zeke I wouldn't stand in your way. I would be right by your side cheering your ass on telling you to jump all on the dick. Why can't I get the same type of support in return.

"Macy, if you and Haze were to have talked about everything and then wanted to get back together I would be your biggest supporter. You can't expect me to support something that doesn't make any sense. This is the first time you are really seeing him and the only thing that happens is you melting into his arms. You want me to support feelings that stirred up all because he held you close. That shit is dumb and I'm not gonna support stupidity. You can get mad all you want but this is me telling you this as a sister."

Haze didn't have to shoot me for me to feel the sensation of the bullets ripping into my body. Eniko's words did the same thing. I just didn't understand why she couldn't be happy for me. Granted we didn't have a conversation but it was going to come later. Right now we were just basking in our glory, which just so happened to be our love.

"Why does a conversation have to matter when feelings are involved. Whether we had the conversation or not the feelings we feel aren't going to change. When he whispered that he missed me I felt whole again. I felt a peace and that was because of him. You can call that stupidity all you want because I call it true love. I don't expect you to understand that though since you will never experience running into your true love again." I hit below the belt but that was only because I wanted to even the score. She hurt me so I had to hurt her.

"YOU FUCKING BITCH!" Eniko screamed before swinging on me. Eniko and I never got into a fist fight with each other before. Her swinging on me and punching me in the face caught me off guard. After a couple of seconds, I pulled my self together and followed up with a couple punches of my own. It took a couple of punches to my face for me to realize that she was really trying to beat my ass. I started fighting for real as we went toe to toe. With every punch I threw Eniko was following up with one of her own.

"Aye, Aye, chill the fuck out." I heard someone say right before a pair of arms wrapped around me pulling me away from Eniko.

"What the hell is going on?" Emanii questioned, looking between the two of us.

"Zeke let me the fuck go so I can black her other fucking eye for busting my lip!" Eniko screamed.

"You shouldn't have been running your mouth. I've always been there for you and the one time I need your support the most you want to act like a bitch. Just know that I owe your ass another fucking beat down for blacking my eye!" I screamed back. I was fuming on the inside pissed the fuck off that she may have given me a black eye.

"Zeke, let me go before I fuck yo ass up. She needs some common sense so I'm going to knock that shit into her dumb ass." Eniko was kicking and swinging trying to get out of the hold that Zeke had her in.

"Zeke, bring her in the house and Haze you take Macy out of here. I can't believe the two of you are fighting at my party." Emanii shook her head as she walked away and I honestly didn't care. Don't get me wrong I felt bad about fighting at her birthday party but the issue that was going on right now was a lot bigger than her damn party. My best friend, my sister, was acting as if I made the worse mistake ever. Haze kept me in his arms until Eniko and Zeke were out of sight.

"Why you out here fighting and shit Macy like you don't go no sense?"

"She doesn't want to be supportive so I was gonna beat that shit into her. Plus she swung on me first."

"That's your sister, which means nothing should come between y'all or bring y'all to blows. She may say she don't support you but no matter what you do she is always going to be there for you because she's your sister. Even if she don't agree with some of your bullshit her ass is always going to be there."

This is what made me fall head over heels for Haze. Eniko had made it clear to both him and me that she wasn't feel our reunion yet he didn't hold it against her. He was truly one of a kind.

"How would you know about my bullshit?"

"You right I wouldn't know because yo ass dipped on a nigga for a whole two years. Then you pop back up with a new nigga by your side." All thirty of his words hit me one after another; they ripped through me as if they were trying to end my life.

"I'm sorry," I whispered.

'No need to apologize I'm over that shit. It's not even important right now," he told me. "You want to go somewhere and talk?" Hearing him bring up me leaving had me feeling like Eniko was right. We needed to have that conversation because I wasn't going to be okay with Haze throwing the fact that I left in my face.

"Yeah, we can get out of here and talk." He grabbed my had and lead me out of the backyard. I wanted to say bye to Emanii and wish her another happy birthday but after the fight I thought it would better to just send her a text.

Haze unlocked his doors and I slide into the passenger seat. As he pulled off I pulled out my phone and text Emanii. Five minutes went passed and she hadn't sent a text back. I made a mental note to call her in the morning and make sure that everything was alright. I turned my phone off ready to give Haze my full attention because nothing else mattered in this moment. I knew things may not be perfect between the two of us in the beginning of us getting back together, but I was willing to work over time to make sure that we were good. It was my mission to make sure that things were perfect between us because the love that we shared was perfect to me. One thing I will say is that when this day started I never pictured me sitting shot gun while my baby speed through the streets of New York.

"You alright over there?" he asked me, looking at me from the corner of his eye.

"Yeah, I'm cool I guess." I giggled.

"What you mean you guess and why you giggling like a school girl?"

"Cause I didn't think when you saw me things would go the way that they did. I honestly thought we were going to get into a big argument or something. I'm just glad that the both of us are being adults about the situation. "

"No lie I didn't think things were going to go this way between us either. When I saw you out in Philly I was ready to end your life on everything. The only reason I didn't was because I would only be hurting myself even more. Just cause you did me dirty doesn't mean the love and care I had for you was going to disappear. We might have been young but the shit we felt was real as fuck and that's on everything."

Nothing needed to be said after Haze said that because he was speaking nothing but the truth. I reach my arm over pinching myself just to make sure that I wasn't dreaming. This whole thing had to be unreal but I wasn't going to question it. I was going to sit here and enjoy myself riding shot with my baby. Whatever nonsense I was gonna have to deal because of my actions I would just deal with them tomorrow. For now, it was all about Haze and I.

* * *

"Pa, slow up you going to fast!" I moaned out.

That talk we were supposed to have never happened. As soon as Haze's front door closed we were all over each other and our clothes soon came off. Haze had me pressed up against the wall with my hands risen over my head and my back arched. His left hand was wrapped snug around my neck while his right hand rest at my hips.

"Ma, you mean to tell me you can't take this dick no mo'?" he grunted.

It took me a second to catch his rhythm but once I did my little ass was poppin' and shaking. My soft moans grew into loud yells. Haze wasn't making love to me like the other dudes had tried to do in the past two years. He was fuckin' the shit out of me and I was loving every minute of it.

"Damn Macy, yo shit still feels good."

He bit into my neck, causing a soft yelp to escape my lips. I used my butt to push him back a little and was able to turn around. I stood there with my back facing the wall and lust filled eyes. My juices were dripping down my leg as Haze dropped to his knees and made a trail from my leg all the way up to where the juices were spilling.

"Ahhhhhhhhh!" I hissed when his lips wrapped around my pearl. He hungrily sucked on it causing my body to erupt in pleasure. This was the greatest feeling I have ever known and I didn't want it to stop. Licking from my entrance to my pearl his thick tongue glided across my pussy. My legs got weak as he moaned into my pussy.

"You taste like peaches, Macy," he hummed against me.

I was going crazy as he treated my pussy like an actually peach. He nibbled, sucked, and slurped until I couldn't take it anymore. My body went into convulsions as Haze had to use his hands to hold me up.

"Fuck, you taste good."

He slurped everything I put out then stood up. He took my left leg wrapped it around his waist, lifted my weak body up a little then shoved his dick back inside of me.

"OHHHHH!" I moaned, wrapping my arms around his neck.

He pumped in and out of me slowly but deep. I felt all of him as my walls tightened around him.

"Don't close your eyes Macy, fucking look at me!" he demanded.

I opened my eyes and stared back into his. I saw a mixture of love and lust in his eyes.

"Macy, do you love me?" he asked slow grinding into me.

"I will always love you," I moaned back.

"No matter what I do?"

"No matter what you do and no matter how far apart we may be. My love for you will always be there. I love you, pa," I told him.

Tears slowly feel from my eyes as I reached my peak at the same time he reached his. Haze leaned forwarded kissing me hungrily feasting on my lips. We stood there kissing each for what seemed like hours until he pulled away from me abruptly.

He smirked at me then walked away from just leaving me there. I stood there for a little while thinking that he went to get something to clean me up. Two minutes turned into five minutes and he still wasn't back. I decided to go look for him and knew exactly where he was when I heard the shower running. Waltzing into the bathroom I slid the glass door back exposing his naked body.

"So you were just going to leave me there while you took a shower?" I questioned.

"Yeah what else did you expect me to do?" The way he was talking was like we didn't just spend the last hour having sex.

"I mean it would've been nice if you would've got something to clean me up with or told me that you were going to take a shower so I could get in with you." I told him.

I went to step in the shower when he reached his hand out stopping me. I looked at him confused because he was acting like he had an issue with me or something.

"What are you doing?"

"I'm trying to get in the shower with you is that a crime."

"Nah, it's not a crime but it's not going to fly either. I need you to get your shit and leave, ma."

*Get my shit and leave.* I repeated to myself.

"Haze what the hell is going on? Why are you acting like this towards me?"

"You like to fuck and leave right? So I fucked you and now you can leave, ma."

"Really!" I spazzed.

"Hell fuckin' yeah. Get the fuck out. I gave your ass what the fuck you wanted and now you can step. Ain't shit here for you anymore Macy. The love I had for you went out the window when you left me when I needed your raggedy ass the most."

"It wasn't my faul—"

"Real shit I don't give a fuck whose fault it was. The story still remains the same that you fucking left me."

"Just let me explain," I cried.

He stepped out the shower, pushed me back then grabbed the towel that was on the rack. "Ain't shit for you to explain cause a nigga don't fucking care. You wanted to fuck and leave so now I'm fucking and kicking you out."

"I'm not going nowhere!" I yelled.

"Macy, I don't have a problem carrying your ass outside naked and throwing yo clothes on the porch. Stop fucking playing with me. Get dressed and get the fuck out."

He scooped me into his arms then brought me back into the living room where our clothes laid across the floor. I he sat me on my feet and I crossed my arms over my bare breast. I wasn't just about to leave out of here. If Haze wanted me to leave then he was gonna have to make me leave.

"Look you either put yo shit on or you go outside naked. The choice is yours."

"No the choice is yours. You are the one kicking me out."

"I don't got time for yo dumb shit." Haze walked away from me and I stood there with a smile on my face. If he thought, it was going to be that easy for him to just fuck then kick me out he had another thing coming.

I sat on the couch and reach for the remote to turn the TV on. While I was flicking through the channels, Haze came back into the living room. He snatched me up forcing me to stand up. The button up he had draped over his shoulder was now on my body and being buttoned up. Haze was doing everything in his power to not look me in the eyes as he buttoned the last button.

"Haze look at me," I told him. My hands reached up to his face but he smacked them away. I tried to touch him again and the same thing happened but this time he pushed my ass against the wall.

"Haze, stop I love you." I told him.

"Fuck all that love shit Macy. Love is for the fucking weak and what happened between the two of us today proved that. I played the love card and yo ass was putty in my fucking hands. I tried to kill yo ass Macy and you forgave me because I said I love you."

"You don't love me?" That was all I got from what he had just said.

"Nah, I don't."

"Then what was all of this for? Why would you act like you wanted me? Why would you act like everything was going to be okay with us when all along yo ass didn't even care about me?" I shouted.

"I wanted to make you feel the pain that I felt for the first year and a half that you left. I wanted you to understand what the fuck that shit did to me. I was ready to play house with yo ass for a couple of months then just leave you high and dry," he confessed.

"Then why didn't you?" I was hoping like hell his answer would've been because he realized just how much he loved me.

"Cause that would be some bitch shit and I'm not a bitch."

"And what you are doing right now doesn't make you bitch?"

"Nah, cause I gave you the same shit that you gave me. It makes me fuckin' even."

"Just let me fuckin' go Haze. I hate yo dumb ass. You think you gave me what I deserved when you don't even fucking know the story. My father fucking took my phone and broke it when I went back home. Then he moved us out of fucking Philly because he didn't want me being with you. I didn't have a choice I was only sixteen at the time. My father watched me closely to make sure that I wasn't in contact with you. He would check my phone on the regular and check my Myspace page and all. You were hurt behind the shit and so was I, unlike you though I didn't allow the hurt that I felt to cause me to act out of character. So yeah I fucking left but I didn't have a choice. You had a fucking choice when you brought me here and you still choose to be a fucked up individual. You don't have to worry about kicking me out because I'll leave on my own. Looking at you right now makes me sick to my stomach."

I snatched my stuff from off the floor and headed for the door. As bad as I wanted to cry I held in the tears because Haze wasn't about to see me sweat. I fucking hated Haze for how he tried break me just now but the love I had for his raggedy ass was still there. When I got outside I called a cab so I could go home and try to forget what happened here tonight. This whole thing had Eniko's words from earlier echoing in my head. I was stupid to believe that Haze would just forgive me so easy. I wasn't even mad at Haze for the stunt he pulled I was mad at myself. I was mad at myself because I allowed him to take me there. I allowed the guilt I felt for leaving him to consume me and make me into a puppet. If I was in my right state of mind then I would've been able to see the hurt that Haze wore on his sleeve instead of being blinded by the love that was in his eyes. He deceived me and this was the last time I was going to allow that to happen. He was mad and hurt right now so I was going to give him his space for now. When I felt it was the right time I was going to make my move on Haze because there wasn't a bitch alive that could love him the way I love him.

## 10: Eniko

"What the hell were the two of you fighting about?" Emanii asked as she passed me some ice wrapped up in a wash cloth.

"I told her that she was being dumb with this whole Haze situation. The last time she saw him he pulled a gun out on her now he wants to be hugged up on him. The she said some slick shit about Liam and I lost it. I honestly don't even want to talk about this anymore." Macy had me pissed off but at the end of the day it was her life not mine. If she wanted to be stupid, then that was on her. I wasn't about to stress myself out behind her decisions.

"I'm not even going to speak on the situation because the both of y'all were wrong. She needs to stop hitting below the belt and you need to let her live her life the way she wants to," Emanii said, shaking her head.

"Baby, come outside so you can open your gifts," Drix said, walking into the kitchen. He came over and wrapped his arms around Manii. Looking at the two of them my heart smiled. They were still going strong and it was a beautiful thing.

"Okay. Eniko, you want to come with me?"

"No I'm okay. I'm about to leave I just need to use your bathroom first."

"It's down that hall and the third door on the right. Call me tomorrow."

"Okay and Happy Birthday again." I got up and gave her a hug, then watched as her and Drix walked out hand in hand.

"Why can't I have something like that?" I questioned aloud. I wasn't envious of what Emanii had, I just couldn't help but to want the same thing. Her and Drix seemed so happy together. That's all I wanted was to be happy with a dude that understood me and wanted nothing more than to see me happy. I shook off the sad feeling that was starting to come over me and headed for the bathroom. Depending on how my lip looked that date with Gavin was gonna have to be postponed.

I got to the bathroom and the door was shut. I didn't think anyone was in there because it seemed quiet. I pushed the door open and saw Zeke standing there with his dick in his hand peeing into the toilet. My eyes feel right on his package and a small gasp escaped my mouth. He was semi hard and the length had to be about five inches. It was thick so it had to extend at least three or four more inches when it was fully hard.

"Ayee! Eniko, do you mind a nigga trying to pee in peace," he said, looking at me.

"Oh I'm sorry," I said quickly closing the door.

A couple of seconds later I heard the water running then Zeke stepped out of the bathroom. I tried to step to the side of him to get into the bathroom but he stepped in front me.

"Uh I'm just trying to get into the bathroom," I told him.

"I'm not stopping you, Eniko." He smiled.

"Um you kind of are." I giggled.

"Why you haven't talked to me all day?" he asked switching the subject.

"I said hi to you when I saw you, Zeke."

"Yeah you said hi but hi is for someone you don't even know. We may not have known each other for long but I think I deserve more than a hi."

"Hey Zeke. Happy now?"

"Nah, I think I need a hug."

"Zeke, I'm not giving you a hug," I told him.

"Why not?"

"Cause I don't want to."

"How old are you again? You talking 'bout cause I don't want to like you five or some shit. Give me a hug and stop playin' girl."

Even though he told me to give him a hug he didn't give me much of a choice. He took my arms wrapped them around his neck then placed his hands at my sides. He squeezed me tight as I fell victim to the smell of his cologne.

"Doesn't this feel right?" he whispered in my ear.

"Mhmmm," I cooed softly. I didn't know what was going on nor did I have control of what my body was doing. I was screaming to myself that this was wrong but my body wasn't paying me any attention.

"Let me taste you, Eniko. You smell good but do you taste good?" He started walking into the bathroom while we were still wrapped up in each other's arms. He let me go and closed the door behind us while I just stood there looking stupid.

He filled up the space that was between us and placed a simple kiss on my lips while he unbuttoned my shorts. Before I knew it my shorts and panties were on the floor and Zeke had my left foot resting on top of the toilet seat. Zeke started off by nibbling on my inner thighs while barely touching me with his fingers.

*Eniko stop this, stop this right now! You know this is wrong. Liam is probably rolling over in his grave behind this. Stop Eniko, please!* I begged myself to stop Zeke from doing the unthinkable but I couldn't physical stop him. My body was his playground and he wasting no time playing. His finger slipped inside of me as Zeke kissed my clit. My body shudder once I felt his lips be replaced by his tongue.

"ZEKE!" I moaned while my chest heaved up and down. He had barely gotten started and my body was acting crazy.

"SHHHHHH!" he whispered. His cool breath against my skin turned me on even more as his fingers dipped and twisted in and out of me.

I held on to his head forcing his face towards my pussy. I worked my hips into his face and he worked his tongue in my middle. I was in sexually bliss as I called out his name. He gripped my thighs as I released my juices into his mouth. He was killing my body softly with his tongue. I quivered as he hummed against my clit. He was driving me crazy as he took my body to height that it's never been to before other than in the dreams that I had recently of Zeke.

He was bringing my sexual fantasies to life and he didn't even know it. The slurping noise along with the moans was driving me crazy. It wasn't long before I was cumming for the second time.

"What the fuck!" I said jumping a little when I felt his finger playing by my booty hole.

"Relax Eniko. I just need to taste you one more time, ma. I need you to cum for me one more time, ight." He looked up at me and his lips were glistening. I wanted to push him away but his eyes were begging me to let him taste me again. This shit was fucking crazy but I allowed him to have his way with me.

It took me a couple of seconds to get used to his finger slipping into my booty hole. Once I warmed up to the feeling the pleasure was indescribable. My body started to squirm as Zeke send waves of pleasure throughout my body over and over again. His lips latched on to my clit and he began sucking it as if he was expecting something to come out of it.

"Eniko," he whispered against my clit.

"Huh?" I said damn near out of breath.

"Let me taste that good good again. Make it wet."

His voice was so smooth and sexy that within seconds of him demanding me to cum I was giving him exactly what he wanted. This time the feeling was more intense. I reached out for the sink and shower curtain to try and steady myself. It felt like my body was vibrating as Zeke cleaned me up with nothing else besides his tongue.

"You ight, ma?" Zeke asked me, standing up. He picked me up and sat me on the bathroom sink. He separated my legs then stood in the middle of them.

"This is so wrong." I said it aloud but I was saying it more to myself.

"What's wrong about it?"

"You are Liam's best friend and I was his girlfriend we shouldn't be messing around like this."

"If Liam was alive this shit would be wrong, but he's not. Don't get me wrong Liam is my nigga and he forever will be but I want you ma. I let you go once and I'm not bout to let you go again."

"You never had me Ezekiel and you never will. This was wrong and I should've stopped you before things even got this far. I have to get out of here," I told him, trying to push him away.

"Stop playing with me. You know you enjoyed what we did as much as I enjoyed being the cause of your body going into convulsions." A smirk appeared on his face causing me to feel disgusted with myself.

"My body enjoyed that but I didn't, Zeke. That shit was dead wrong and you know it. Now move the hell out of my way so I can go about my business."

He ignored what I said slipped his hands on the side of my face then forced me to kiss him. I tried to fight him off but when his tongue slipped inside my mouth all of those feelings I felt for Zeke came rushing back. The feelings I felt when I first saw him all the way to the feelings I felt when he played my young ass to the left. The all hit me at once causing me to give in to the kiss. I kissed him like I needed him more than anything on this earth. It was so intense that when he pulled away I jumped off the bathroom sink and pulled him back into the kiss.

"You can fight it all you want but being with me is where you want to be. I'm not going to force you into a relationship with me Eniko but I'm not going to let you be without me either. Get dressed and get out of here. I'll call you tomorrow," he told me after he ended our kiss for the second time.

When he left out the bathroom I stayed in there trying to pull myself together. Nothing was making sense to me right now and all I wanted was some understanding. A part of me knew messing with Zeke was wrong, then the other side of me craved him. I craved him the same way Pinocchio craved to be a real boy. The whole situation was crazy because I had just got on Macy for falling for Haze so quickly and here my fast ass was getting head in the bathroom. Zeke helped me to experience pleasure in a way I never experienced before.

Trying to shake any thoughts of Zeke I slipped on my panties and pulled my shorts on. I left out of the bathroom quick and in a hurry. I rushed out the house making sure I didn't run into anyone. I went straight to my car got in and drove off like a bat out of hell.

"It was just a one-time thing it doesn't mean anything and it will never happen again. Chalk it up to you not having sex in a while and temptation being a bitch. That's it and that's all," I said aloud, trying to make myself believe the words I just said. I thought if I said it aloud it would help me believe that what I did was a mistake, only it didn't. Nothing about what Zeke and I did felt like a mistake but I knew it was wrong. Which meant I needed to keep my distance from Zeke cause it was obvious he was able to speak a language only him and my body understood.

\* \* \*

"What happened to you being ready at eight?" I heard his voice as soon as I was about to put my key in the door. I turned around slowly trying to get myself together.

"Heyyy!" I tried to say it regular but it came out all high pitched in funny.

"You sound sneaky as hell Eniko. Wassup?"

"Nothing."

He came closer to where I stood and gazed down at me. Since I was a lot shorter than he was I refused to look up at him.

"When I'm talkin' to you, you look me in the eyes. Never lower your head in a presence of a man and especially not me," he told me, cupping my chin then lifting my head.

"Eniko, I'm only going to ask you this once and I don't want to hear no bullshit story about you walking into a door or some shit."

"I wouldn't even tell you anything like that. I got into it with Macy. It's nothing serious but that's why I was late."

"I know that's your girl and all but I hope her lip look worse than yours cause if not I'ma have to get you some boxing gloves and teach you a thing or two."

"That's not funny at all."

"It may not be funny to you cause you got the busted lip but that shit is funny, ma."

"Whatever I'm going in the house. I'll see you later," I told him and unlocked the downstairs door.

"Aye, hol' up, we supposed to be going on a date."

"I'm not going out with my lip looking like this."

"Then our date can be here. You thought I was just going to let off the hook that easy? I waited long enough for yo ass to go on a date with me so we about to go inside you gonna order some pizza and we gonna watch something up in that bitch," he said.

"I guess we can do that." I playfully rolled my eyes.

"Roll them funky ass eyes all you want to but a nigga was going upstairs whether you said yes or not." I grabbed his hand leading him up to the apartment slightly laughing at the funny shit he said.

I wasn't sure where things were going to go with Gavin and I wasn't pressed for them to go anywhere. All I wanted was for Gavin to distract me enough to where Zeke wouldn't have an effect on me. I needed to rid myself of Zeke because him and I being together just wasn't the right move. Today proved that he was good for my body but was toxic for my soul. Zeke and I would never be and that was something he was gonna have to learn.

# *11: Macy*

For the past week the tension around the house has been so thick you couldn't even cut it with a knife. Eniko wasn't talking me and I wasn't talking to her. Matter of fact I wasn't talking to anyone and the only person I did want to talk to was Haze. Haze did me dirty that night he sexed me then kicked me out. If he was any other nigga I probably would've slit his tires or something by now, but he wasn't any other nigga he was Haze. Even though it wasn't my fault I still hurt Haze and it makes sense that he wanted to even the score. Now that the score was even I wasn't up for any more games. I was determined to get things back right with us because deep down I knew the two of us were soulmates. Haze was it for me and no one could tell me anything different. I didn't care what I had to do by the time I started school in the fall Haze and I were going to be on the right track.

"Can I talk to you, Macy?" Eniko asked when she saw me go into the kitchen to get a bottle of water. She was sitting on the couch watching *Maury*, which is something we usually did together. Eniko and I never stopped talking for more than two days. Us not talking for a week was bothering me but I damn sure wasn't going to cave in. The things she said to me hurt and I wanted an apology. If she was willing to apologize, then I would do the same and we could act like none of this happened.

"I didn't know we had something to talk about. We haven't talked for the past week."

"I'm not even going to feed into the bs if you want to talk and put what happened between us behind us then let me know. I'm not going to beg you to talk to me."

"No one said you had to beg. I'm just saying I didn't know we had something to talk about." I was being a bitch to her because her ass deserved. Yes, I said some fucked up things but what she said caused me to come out the side of my neck. Her actions caused a reaction and now she had to deal with the consequences.

"Forget I even said anything because I'm not trying to go there with you again. How's that eye healing up?" she spoke sarcastically. I caught what she was saying and laughed to myself because it was a good one.

"Just cause you caught me off guard and blacked my eye the first time doesn't mean you can do it again. I'm so tired of your stuck up ways, Eniko. What the hell happened to the full of life sister that I used to have? What happened to the sister that would never judge me? What happened to us always being there for each other whether we were in the right nor in the wrong. I don't even know who you are anymore nor do I even care to find out." I stood there glaring at her while I tapped my foot trying to calm myself down.

"I'm sorry I'm not the same girl I was two years ago before the love of my life died. I'm working on myself and that's all I can fucking do, Macy. I can't just go from being happy and in love to being depressed to being back happy and looking for love. It doesn't work that way with me. I'm trying the best that I can to be more open to things but it's hard. I may have said a lot of things to you that night about Haze but I wasn't judging you. I was simple trying to get you to realize that if you and Haze are going to work it's going to take more than a couple of I miss you's. Regardless of it all I was still going to support your decision because at the end of the day I love you and you're my sister. I know I hurt your feelings and I apologize for that because that was never my intensions."

"I appreciate the apology and I apologize for bringing up Liam. I may never understand the hurt you felt when Liam died but I can't keep bringing it up. You will get over it in your own time. "

'Come give me a hug." She smiled getting off the couch. She walked towards me with her arms stretched out.

"Eniko move, we are not kids anymore. We don't need to hug it out."

"Shut up and give me a hug." She forced me into a hug and after a second I gave in.

"So what have I missed for the past week. It can't be much since you don't do much," I told her.

"You stay taking slick jabs at me like I'm this boring chick that does nothing but complain and nag."

"That's kind of what you are." I laughed.

"Let you tell it I am, that's not here nor there though. When I went into the house after you left I went to the bathroom to see how bad my lip looked. Thanks for the busted lip by the way."

"You're welcome if I was walking away with the black eye then you had to be marked up too."

"Whatever. Listen though, Zeke happened to be in the bathroom and when I walked in I saw his package."

"Wait what?" I asked fully interested in the story now, not that I wasn't interested when she started but whenever her name and Zeke's name were in the same sentence something juicy was to follow.

"I saw it and even though it wasn't all the way hard he was still a good length. Somehow we both ended up in the bathroom and he blessed me with the greatest gift I ever received." She bit her lip and quivered a little when she said it. With a screwed face, I just stared at her for a second.

"Ewww did you just cum on yourself?" I asked serious as hell.

"Bitch no, but if I did I wouldn't even be mad at myself. Macy when I say his tongue worked wonders it worked wonders. I was almost on the verge of tears at one point. It was euphoric and I can't keep his ugly ass out of my mind." She sighed grabbing a pillow and throwing it over her face.

"You know damn well Zeke isn't ugly. Why are you fighting the feeling with him anyway? I say if his tongue brought you that much pleasure then use him for pleasure only." I shrugged.

"I'm not about to use him for sex."

"Why not? Men use woman for sex all the time."

"For one he was one of Liam's best friends and two Gavin has been occupying my time."

"Okay for one you were into Zeke before you were into Liam and Liam didn't have a problem stepping to you. Zeke gave Liam his blessing so I'm sure Liam would understand if you messed around with Zeke. Two Gavin is just occupying your time that doesn't mean you are tied down. It's the summer and we just graduated high school. I say date them both then figure out which one you want to be with by the end of the summer. At least that way you won't have no regrets about what you may have missed out on with one of them."

"Ehh, I don't know."

"I say go for what it. You wanna start living, well now is your time. I'm not saying you have to sleep with the both of them. I'm just saying date the two of them and see where it goes. It's obvious you have sexual chemistry with Zeke so see if you have any other chemistry with him. Gavin is feeling you and you are somewhat feeling him so give him a chance too."

She sat there looking at me I guess trying to figure out if I was serious and I was. Eniko was young and had been through a lot a young age. Now she was at a new stage in her life and she needed to embrace it and embrace herself.

"You know what as crazy as your idea may sound I think I'm going to try it. I keep telling myself that I am going to reinvent myself and move on from the past but I never do it. Yes, I still care for Liam but I can't let his death define me. I have to live my life while I'm amongst the living because I don't want to regret it when I'm dead. Like you said Gavin is just occupying my time, I'm not tied down nor do I have a ring on my finger."

"That's right Eniko!" I cheered her on.

"Next time Zeke steps to me I'm going to play it cool. I'm going to act uninterested but giving him enough to where he keeps trying."

"And what about Gavin?"

"He went back to Philly after our date so I won't be seeing him no time soon I think. I'll just continue to text and call him."

"That's my girl. Just make sure not to get caught up."

"Me caught up, never," she said, waving me off but I knew better.

"Well since we are talking about our plans for the summer, I plan on making Haze mine."

"So things went well between the two of you when you left?"

"I wouldn't say things went well but I got a look into some things."

"Be real with me Macy. What happened?"

"You were right just because we said I miss you didn't mean that everything was right between the two of us. He took me back to his place, we had sex then he kicked me out."

"Are you okay? I knew he wasn't shit. You deserve so much better Macy, fuck him."

"No you got it all wrong. I don't deserve better I deserve him. This is something that you're not going to understand and I don't want to be judged for it. All I want is your support, Eniko."

"I'll support you but I'm letting you know right now I don't like what he did to you. How is he going to sweet talk you, sleep with you, and then kick you out?"

"I mean it's a lot better than what he planned on doing."

"What did he plan on doing?"

"He was going to lead me on for months then just disappear on me the same way I did him."

"Macy—"

"Eniko no! I don't want to hear how I didn't deserve what he put me through because I feel like I did deserve it."

"You don't even have to explain because it's not meant for me to understand nor do I need an explanation. What are you going to do now?"

"Well he's not the happiest with me and I saw how much I actually hurt him so the only thing left for me to do is make it up to him."

"How are you supposed to do that? I mean I'm sure he doesn't want to talk to you."

"He doesn't have to want to talk to me for me to talk to him. The same way that these dudes be pressed when they are trying to bag a chick is the same way I'm about to pressed for him. I'm going to make it to where he can't help but to get back with me."

"If that's what you want to do then you have my full support."

"Good cause I'm going to need your help. With you dating Zeke, Haze will have no choice but to see me."

"Hold on, I'm not going to rush into dating Zeke because you want to use us to get back with Haze. I'm going to handle Zeke very differently. I'm not the fourteen-year-old girl who he kissed and then broke my heart."

"Well alright then who are you then boo," I told her ampin' her up.

"I'm not sure, but I know who I'm not and that's all that matters." She laughed.

"It was a start," I told her, laughing too.

"I'm glad we got things back on the right track. I missed you this week."

"Awww you can't go a day without me how cute," I told her.

"Don't hype yourself. I don't want to rain on our parade but what are you going to do about Rex?"

"I'm going to break things off with him. I just haven't figured out if I want him to come here or if I want to go out there."

"I say do it here so if things go south you can just kick his ass out."

"Or I can just do it there and leave after I do it."

"Whichever works for you, just make sure that you do it before you even step to Haze."

"I will."

"I'm about to go meet up with Emanii. She's bored at home and wanted me to come over," Eniko told me.

"Oh so I stop talking to you and Emanii for a week and y'all just stop including me in things."

"It's hard to include you in anything when you don't answer the phone."

"Whatever I'm coming so wait for me to get dressed and we can go over there together."

"Just make it quick."

"I'm not about to rush I have to take my time just in case I see my boo," I told her, getting off the couch and heading towards my room.

Fixing things with Eniko wasn't the first thing on my to do list but I'm glad we talked it out. I'm even more happier that she is ready to start living life. I would've never guessed she would've took my advice about dating two men at the same time. This was new for her but I think it's going to be good for her and hopefully at the end of the summer she would choose Zeke. It wasn't that I didn't like Gavin I just always felt Zeke was the person for Eniko. I just never said anything because I could want something for her but if she didn't want it for herself then it made no sense to speak on it.

I couldn't worry about Eniko's situation too much because I had a situation of my own. I was in full operation get my man back and I only had about six weeks to do it. I needed Haze back in my life before I started school because my studies were going to be taking up a lot of my time. Dealing with Haze wasn't going to be easy and I was perfectly fine with that. My father would always tell me that nothing worth having comes easy which made me believe all the trouble I knew I was going to get into because of Haze was gonna be worth it.

## 12: Emanii

"All I'm asking is for you to think about. What's so wrong with you thinking about me going to Columbia?"

"I thought about it Manii and I'm not for it. You are about to have a baby in three and a half. What are you going to do when you have to take time off in the middle of the semester to have a baby! You may think I'm doing this just to tell you what to do when I'm telling you this because I have your best interest at heart, ma. I don't want you to get into school and then have to drop out because of the baby. That shit isn't going to do nothing but make you regret having the baby in the first place."

"Do you really think that I'm the type of chick that would regret having their baby? I don't care how much I may struggle with school because I'm a teenage mother. I will never and I mean never regret my child. I'm not the sick person that raised you, Hendrix!"

"The fuck you just say to me!" The face that I learned to love wasn't the same face I was staring at in this moment. Everything happened so fast that I didn't realize he smacked me until I felt the sting of his hand connecting with my cheek.

"Nigga, did you just put your fucking hands on me!" I shouted. I pushed him as hard as I could trying to shove his ass away from me.

"Don't throw that bitch in my face, Manii. You know the shit I've been through. I shouldn't have put my hands on you but you was wrong for saying that shit."

"Fuck you and that bitch! You wanna put your hands on me, I'ma show your ass what kind of bitch I am." I stormed passed him waltzing into my kitchen. I pulled the biggest butcher knife I had in my drawer and charged towards Drix. I only managed to graze him with the knife before he snatched it from my hand.

"The fuck you doing, Manii? Chill the fuck out," he told me.

"No you get the fuck out Drix. How dare you fucking raise your hand to me all because I brought up your bitch of a mother." I was pacing back and forth trying to figure out how I was going to kill this muthafucker without getting caught.

"I said it was my bad. You taking shit to the next level cutting me and shit."

"You took shit to the next level when you put your hands on me, Hendrix. You should know me better than anyone and you know I don't tolerate that shit. Just get the fuck out my house before a coroner has to take your body the fuck out of here."

"You really gonna act like that, Emanii?" I looked at this nigga like he asked the stupidest question in the world.

"Hendrix, I may be eighteen but trust me I am wise beyond my years. I will not put up with you putting your hands on me. You do that shit once then I'm sure your ass can do it twice. Just get out before things go further then it need too."

"Fine. I love you, Manii." He kissed me on the cheek sat the knife on the table then headed for the door.

I was tempted to pick that knife up and throw it at the back of his head. I sided against it because I had another life to think about. Not to mention a bitch was built for a lot of things but jail wasn't one of them. Tears came to my eyes as I thought about what was in store for my life. Columbia was my dream and when I got in I couldn't have been happier. Right after finding out I got in I found out that I was pregnant. Everything Drix said earlier were things that I already thought about which was why I was alright with not going and just going to a community college. After talking to Eniko for the past week about the situation things changed and she helped me find the courage to go to Columbia. The only problem was Hendrix wasn't trying to budge on the idea.

It hurt that he didn't think I was capable of going to school and being a mother. If anyone was supposed to believe in me, it was supposed to be Hendrix. I have been there for him ever since he told me about the things his mother was putting him through. Shit, I was even the one to pull the trigger and kill her ass. I did it out of love which should've been the same reason Hendrix encouraged me to go to Columbia. With him putting his hands on me, I honestly didn't care anymore for his support. Even if I had to defer for a year I was going to go to Columbia and prove his dumb ass wrong.

I left out the kitchen and went into the bathroom to look at my cheek in the mirror. He didn't leave a mark but my cheek was red. I shook my head and wiped away the tears because I refused to cry behind his ass. When my mother got ill I ended up growing tough skin. In a way my innocence was stripped from me and I had to grow up fast. I didn't have a mother figure to talk to about sex, boys, and other womanly things that you encounter in high school. I had to deal with it alone and I one of the things I taught myself was to never allow a man to walk all over me nor put his hands on me. Hendrix is the love of my life so I wasn't letting him off the hook so easily, but he wouldn't be coming back to stay in our house for a while.

The ringing of my phone caused me to rush out the bathroom and stump my toe on the kitchen table. I stood there in pain while answering the phone.

"Ugh hello."

"Why you sound so ugly?" Macy asked.

"Shut up I stumped my toe trying to get to the phone and it hurts like hell. Where are you and Eniko? Y'all was supposed to be here an hour ago."

"That's why I'm calling, we've been knocking on your door for the last three minutes."

"My bad I'm coming now."

I rushed over to the front door opening it for my girls. After going into the kitchen to get some snacks and drinks we sat on the living room floor the same way we did back in the day.

"Why is your face red, Manii?" Eniko asked.

Unconsciously I raised my hand and gently touched my cheek. When I touched it I felt the pain Drix hand caused angering me all over again.

"Drix slapped me because I brought up his mother. Now before any of you say something about me being in the wrong for doing that I already know. I'm not going to apologize for it though. He made it seem like I was going to be this horrible mother if I went to Columbia."

"Did he say you would be a horrible mother or did you come to that conclusion on your own?" Macy questioned.

"He said that me going to school then having to drop out because of the baby was going to make me regret my child. How could someone who has known me all my life say something like that. I don't matter how hard things get I would never regret my child. I laid down, opened my legs and allowed him to slid into me without a condom. I allowed him to do all of that which means I have to lay in the bed I mad. This baby is probably going to be the greatest thing that ever happened to me, so why do I have to give up everything just to be a mother!" I sobbed.

I didn't mean to start crying it was just all hitting me. I wanted to be superwoman and I believed that I could be. At only eighteen I have killed, lost my mother and my brother at the same time, and I was able to bounce back from that. Having this baby wasn't going to be any different. I just couldn't understand how Drix couldn't see it that way.

"So he put his hands on you because you want to go to school? Emanii, fuck that nigga!"

"Macy, shut up."

"No I'm not going to shut up. Any dude that doesn't commend his woman for wanting to go to school, even while pregnant, is a dumbass. If I was you I would leave that nigga alone and handle my business on my own."

"Don't listen to Macy because she doesn't know anything. What Drix did was messed up and you shouldn't just allow him back in your life so easily, but you shouldn't kick him out of your life either. Y'all have a baby on the way so the rules are different. As far as the school thing goes I still believe that you should go. Your mother can help out and so can Drix," Eniko told me.

"When it comes to me attending Columbia that's not up for debate. I was just asking Drix to think about it but after he put his hands on me, I plan on going there whether he is okay with it or not. As far as me leaving him that's not going to happen neither is me welcoming him back home with open arms. That nigga is gonna have to work to get back in my good graces."

I laughed trying to lighten up the mood. The two them coming over here was supposed to be a happy thing but because of my drama it turned foul as soon as they walked in the door.

"Making people work to be in their good graces must be something that runs in the family." Macy smiled.

"What made you say that?" I was a bit confused as to where she was going with this.

"Haze played her and now she plans on working double time to make him realize the two of them are meant to be together," Eniko explained.

"I should've known something was up with Haze. We had a family dinner like a week before my birthday and when we told him you were coming to my birthday his ass left before I could even make his plate. Him coming to my birthday was a surprise to me but the even bigger surprise was the two of you all hugged up on each other. Haze doesn't forgive easily you sure you want to try and fix things with him. He's not the same person that he used to be." Haze has turned cold these last couple of years. He didn't give a fuck about anyone else's family besides mines, Zeke's, and Drix's. If you weren't the three of us then that nigga would shoot yo ass first and ask questions never.

"Is the sky blue and is Lemon still a sour as bitch?" Macy asked giggling.

"Yes to the both of them. Lemon has become even more of a sour bitch," I told them.

"Alright then my answer is hell yes. Haze may not be the person he used to be and I'm okay with that. Hell, I'm not the same person either. He wants to make me fight for his love then that's what I'm going to do. We make boys fight for us all the time I think it's about time we switch up the roles."

"Don't say I didn't warn you," I told her with a shrug of my shoulders.

"Don't warn me because just like I told Eniko you are going to help me. You are his cousin which means you should know his whereabouts."

"Okay—"

"Just tell me where he is going to be tonight and I will handle the rest."

"There is supposed to be a block party out on 125$^{th}$ that they are going to. I was going to slide through later if the two of you want to come."

"We are coming." Macy cheesed.

"Speaking of Lemon what is her status with your brother?" Eniko asked.

"Since when did you become interested in my brother?"

"Him and I had an interesting conversation in your bathroom the day of your party."

"You don't even have to say anymore. From what I know him and Lemon aren't dating any more. They dated on and off for the past two years but it was never nothing serious, at least for Zeke it wasn't."

"That's good to know. I'll make it my business to run into him at the block party." She smiled before picking up her phone.

"I just want to say that I love the two of you girls like sisters but both Haze and Zeke are my family. I don't know exactly what the two of you got going on with Gavin and Rex, but all I know is I don't want Zeke nor Haze getting hurt."

"Do you really think we would put them into some mess?" Eniko asked as if she was hurt by what I told her.

"I'm not saying that the two of you will I'm just saying that it can happen. Rex is a street dude and even though I don't know how he handles things, him losing you to another dude may not go over well. Gavin seems cool but again I don't know him either. All I'm saying is I don't want no shit coming from them Philly dudes so if Haze and Zeke are what the two of you want then by all means go after them. If not then leave them be."

I wanted to say more about the Gavin and Zeke situation but instead I left it alone. I said my peace about the situation, only time would tell if what I said had stuck with them. I knew Macy and Eniko weren't some snake bitches, but I wouldn't be me if I didn't warn them about my family. I would kill behind Drix, Zeke, and Haze. They have always been there for me, which meant I was always going to be there for them. I wasn't a killer but when it came to my family I would do whatever to make sure that they all remained safe and out of harm's way.

## *13: Haze*

"Why every time we have a meeting yo ass wants to walk in here late like we not on a time schedule. Lateness means slow money and I'm not in the business of slow money which means yo ass needs to be on time," I told Dean.

"Haze you always talkin' big shit like I wasn't the nigga that put you on to the fast money. I don't work on anyone else's time but my own, nigga."

"Dean we all know you're a pussy so cut the big boy act and just tell us why you called this meeting?" I laughed. It wasn't nothing for me and Dean to get into it whenever we had a meeting. His ass was always coming in late and I always had something to say about it.

"Look, Mitch has been watching the way y'all little niggas been doing business and he's impressed. What y'all say about being the distros for all of New York?"

I nodded my head weighing my options as I waited for Zeke to speak up. We were all leaders in our own right but when it came to handling business with Dean, Zeke was always the one to speak up on opportunities.

"That's not something I can answer right now. We're a team which means we have to discuss this as a team," Zeke told him.

"That's why y'all young niggas are going to make it far in this game. Y'all don't act on impulse and y'all discuss things among each other. Even though Zeke is the one that speaks up whenever comes to business I know he don't make the decisions alone. I may not have been too fond of y'all niggas when I first met y'all but I'm proud of you."

"Oh shit this nigga Dean has a soul," Drix joked.

"Do I need to set yo ass up again with a fake robbery?" Dean joked back.

"Don't play like that my nigga, shit is different now. Whoever you send will get laid down. My murder game is real now a days, ask about me," Drix boasted.

"Let me get the fuck out of here before I have to lay one of you cocky niggas down. Y'all have until August 31st to make a decision on the distro move. If y'all agree to it then all three of you will be able to meet the man who will be making y'all rich before y'all turn twenty-five." Dean dapped us all up then left out of the warehouse that we were in leaving us to our thoughts. In the years that we have been working for Mitch we have had numerous phone calls with the nigga but have yet to see him in the flesh.

"So what y'all think about what this nigga said?" Drix asked.

"I've been thinking about the shit for a minute but I was going to keep it under wraps until we turned twenty-one. We got into this shit just to make us enough money to fix our old situations. Our situations are fixed but we ain't do nothing legit with our money yet. Trying to do anything at the age of twenty is going to be hard cause questions are going to be asked about where the money is coming from."

"Zeke's got a point I know this ain't supposed to be the end goal but shit when life give's you lemons we ain't got no choice but to make lemonade." I chuckled. "No pun intended Zeke."

"Nigga, you know what you were doing by saying that bitch shit." Zeke laughed

"Drix, how do you feel about it? You got a baby on the way so if anyone's opinions matters it would be yours," I told him.

Us becoming distro's would put Drix in harm's way, which could possible mean my little cousin growing up without a father. I wasn't about to sit here and tell a grown ass man what to do, and on the other hand I wouldn't be mad if he wanted to sit this one out.

"Being a distro means more money so I'm down for it. I got a kid on the way and yeah I'm good right now and shit, I just don't know how much longer that's going to last. From what I hear kids are expensive and I want to give mines everything he or she deserves. So if y'all down for a being distro's then I'm down. Ain't no way I'm going to take the sucker way out anyway."

"Ight then. With us moving up that means people in our camps have to move up. Only the loyal and strong survive. From now until August we take whomever doesn't seem to be a part of the team. The larger we get the smaller our circle has to be. I'm not taking no chances getting to the top just to be takin' down by someone on our teams. Anyone that looks suspicious will get laid the fuck down," Zeke said.

"In addition to what Zeke said we have to start moving smarter. I'm not saying we was out here making stupid moves but we have to wisen up. Not only will niggas in the street be trying to take us down once they get wind of our come up but also the feds will be coming into play. Each one of us can handle our own in jail if it ever comes down to it, the point is to not let it come down to it. We out here to get money and nothing else. Any dumb moves that happen we lay the nigga who made the move done. We are only as strong as our weakest link and I don't know about y'all two niggas but I ain't fucking weak."

I was talking as if I was talking to a room full of niggas when in reality I was only talking to Zeke and Drix. Just like Zeke wanted us to kill off anyone in our camp that wasn't up to par, I wanted us to kill anyone who moved funny or who made dumb ass moves. I wasn't about to get caught slippin' because of anyone else.

"I hear where the both of y'all coming from, but it's a beautiful day out and we have a block party to be getting' to. All this killin' shit can wait until tomorrow. Y'all act like killin' is the only fucking thing y'all know how to do," Drix joked.

"Nigga like you don't be right there with us guns out blazing." I got out my chair and headed for the exit of the warehouse.

"I never said that I wasn't. Y'all niggas just take killing people to a whole new level. I kill when I have to, Zeke kills when he feels like he needs to teach someone a lesson or make an example out of someone. You though, my nigga you kill for the fuckin' sport of that shit. If there was a killing Olympics, you would get a gold medal every fucking time."

"Drix, shut the fuck up. Y'all heading to the block party now or y'all going back to the crib first."

"I'm going straight there," Zeke said.

"Me too I'm not trying to go back to the crib. Manii and I got into it and that shit didn't end too well."

"What happened? Shit probably wasn't even that big of an issue," I asked.

Drix and Manii were always arguing about some dumb shit. Even though they argued often they never let the little shit they were going through stop them from going home to the other. Now that Drix mentioned he had got into an argument with Manii it made sense why his phone wasn't glue to his hand.

"I don't even want to talk about that shit. I'm going to give her some time to get over it. We gonna be back to normal come tomorrow."

"You know how my sister can be, just get her some food and she will be straight," Zeke told him. "You riding with me and leaving your car here or you gonna drive up to 125th on your own?"

"I'm a drive cause I don't want to be left stranded when you bringing a bitch home."

"The only chick I'm trying to bring home is Eniko. If it ain't her then I'm not fucking with no one."

"How is things going with her?" I asked out of curiosity.

Sex with Macy has been on my mind heavy since I had her at the crib. I tried messing with other females to keep thoughts of Macy to a minimum and that shit only made it worse. No one's insides felt as good as Macy's, she had me addicted and the shit wasn't healthy for me or her.

"I gave her a week to get her shit together."

"She went for that?" Drix asked.

"It don't matter what she went for cause her ass ain't got no choice. I fucked up when I chose Lemon over her ass. Sitting back and watching Eniko with Liam killed me but there wasn't shit I could do about it. I have a chance to do the right thing so that's what I'm going to do even if I have to kidnap her ass."

"I don't think kidnapping her is your second chance but to each his own, my nigga. Let's get out of here I'm hungry as fuck," Drix said, walking out.

"You gonna meet us there, right?" Zeke asked me.

"Yeah I'ma just ride my bike over there," I told them.

I dapped them up then got on my bike and sped off. Zeke was a better nigga then I could ever be. I didn't believe in that second chance shit. Macy had one chance and she fucked up. I wished shit could be different between us, I just didn't know how that could be. Everything I am today is because of her. She couldn't go back and rewrite history making everything that happened forever etched in stone. I will say that I didn't feel the need to cause her misery or pain. The same way I couldn't allow myself to bring her pain that night is the same way I was feeling now. Her little boyfriend was still going to catch my bullets though. It was the principle. He pulled a gun out on me and didn't kill me, which meant I had to kill him for even feeling like it was okay to pull out on me. Like I said before it was just the principle of the streets shit wasn't personal.

\* \* \*

Everyone came out to the annual 125th block party and this year was no different. Mothers, grandmothers, kids, baby mommas, girlfriends, and hood rats were all on the block partying it up like it 1995. Zeke, Drix, and I parked in the middle of the block party making sure that where we stood gave us the ability to see everything in every direction. Even though we didn't frequent Harlem too often niggas still knew of us; when a nigga knew of you that left room for a jaggin'. I wasn't too keen about people sneaking up on me so wherever I went I made sure that I was able to see everything around me.

"Haze, when are you going to give me a chance to show you what real love feels like?" Rose flirted, standing in front of me.

"I tried that real love shit, it wasn't for me and if it was you wouldn't be the candidate for me."

"You trying to say I'm not your type?" she reached out, caressing my cheek and I slapped her hand away.

"Nah, I'm saying you everyone's type and that's the problem. I'ma give you a word of advice, keep yo hands off of me and work on deleting yo hoe card. You delete that shit you might be able to bag a nigga that would wife you."

"Fuck you, Haze!"

"I'm cool on that, ma." I laughed watching her walk away. As if a kinetic force was pulling us together, my eyes went from Rose to staring into Macy's beautiful eyes. Manii, Eniko, and Macy walked towards us and our eyes weren't the only ones on them. They stopped any movement that was going as they passed, the shit was crazy. Macy was rocking a short jumper that had the pockets hanging out of the bottom. A pair of jay's adorned her feet and her top was nothing but a sports bra. One strap went over her shoulder while the other one hung lose. Her soft baby doll curls framed her face giving her an angelic look. I wasn't even trying to fuck with her but the way she was looking was making it hard not to.

"Zeeky!" I heard Manii say.

"Sis, you just can't be jumping all on me anymore. You bigger than me now."

"Did you just call me fat?"

"Manii come on, now you know those words didn't come out my mouth. Wassup Macy. Eniko, come here ma," Zeke said.

"Haze, you're just going to let him call me fat," Manii said to me.

"You know you not fat Manii. The baby just enhances your beauty," I told her all the while still staring at Macy. She was standing next to Manii and I couldn't take my eyes off of her.

"Hey Haze, I just want to say that we all good," Eniko said. I finally tore my eyes away from Macy to look at her.

"You sure I don't want to hug you and then you try and fight me and shit."

"We good," she said. I got up giving her a hug along with Emanii. I hit Macy with a head nod then went back to leaning on the car.

"Ummmm Zeke come take Eniko and I to get something to eat," Manii said.

"Ight, Drix you coming?"

"No Zeeky I asked you to take us, not his ass," Manii sassed.

"I don't care who you asked. I'm coming with you in case one of these niggas try to act stupid," Drix told Manii.

"What you gonna do slap them the way you slapped me?"

"You did what?" Zeke spat, yoking Drix up.

I stood up with my arms folded waiting for Drix to explain what the hell Manii just said. Drix is my nigga but wasn't no one about to put his hands on her.

"Zeeky let him go it wasn't even that serious," Emanii said.

"Nigga, you puttin' your hands on my sister? I gave yo ass my blessin' to date her not fucking hit her!" Zeke spat, punching Drix in the face. Manii tried to jump on Zeke but I grabbed her before she could.

"Chill out Manii that nigga shouldn't have been putting his hands on you," I told her.

"I don't need you two fight my battles. I will handle what Drix did on my own. Zeeky you punched him that's enough."

"You lucky you about to be a father and you're my boy. Put your hands on my sister again and shit ain't going to be so sweet." Zeke let Drix go then stormed off. Emanii followed behind her brother and Eniko went with her.

"Man Haze let me explain that shit—" Drix started but I put my hand up silencing him.

"Ain't shit for you to say, my nigga. No matter what she did your hands should've never been raised to her."

"I hear you, my nigga. I'm about to get out of here I ain't even feeling this shit anymore."

"Yeah you do that," I told him.

I shook my head as I watched Drix hop into his car and pull off. This shit was going to cause some tension within the group I could see the shit now.

"You're not going to say anything to me?" she asked, standing in front of me with her hip poked out.

"Sup," I told her.

"Heyyyy Haze," a chick sang walking past. I didn't know who she was but I grabbed her and pulled her in between my legs.

"Wassup ma, who told you to come out here dressed like that?" I tugged at her dress with one hand while running my other hand across her chin.

"I only wore it to catch your attention," she cooed eye fucking me. Shawty was alright lookin' but if Macy wouldn't have been standing here her ass wouldn't have caught my attention on her best day.

"Um excuse me you do see me standing here, right?" Macy asked the chick forcing her to turn around by her shoulder.

"Does it look like I care and next time keep your hands to yourself. Now back to you, baby." The chick smiled turning back to me.

"Haze, you have two minutes to get this dog face bitch out your face or I will do it for you," Macy threatened.

"Don't pay her no mind, ma. What you doing after this is over?"

The girl was steady talking but my focus wasn't on her. I was looking past her and staring at Macy as she started counting aloud. Her ass was really standing here counting to a hundred and twenty. I shook my head and gave the girl back my attention.

"I'm trying to go where ever you are… arghhhhh!!!!"

Macy had this girl by her hair dragging her away from me.

"I asked you did you see me standing there right and yo ass wanted to act like I was invisible. I bet yo ugly ass see's my invisible ass now. If I catch you around my man again I will do something far worse than dragging your ass in public. If you think I'm playing just fucking try me. Matter of fact this should teach your ass a lesson." Macy picked her foot up and kicked her in the face twice. I grabbed her in a bear hug and walked with her the short distance to my car.

"This the second time in less than a month that yo ass is out here fighting like you don't know better. You're above this fighting shit ma and you need to start acting like it," I told her. I was leaned up against my bike and she was standing in between my legs. I had my arms around her waist making sure she didn't go nowhere.

"Oh now you have something to say to me? I told you to get that bitch out of your face before I did it for you. You wasn't paying me no mind then and now I beat her ass, you want to act like you care. Miss me with the dumb shit Haze," Macy sassed. Her going off on me caused the attraction I already felt for her to grow. I wasn't trying to fuck with her but like I said before she was making it hard not to.

"You wanted my attention and now you got it. Stop acting like this ain't what you want," I told her.

"You're what I want and I plan on having you. What I'm not going to do is fight every chick over you."

"Where's your little boy at?" I reached out touching the heart pendant I got her for her fifteenth birthday. I was surprised that she still had it and amused she decided to wear it today.

"What little boy?" She had the screw face causing a smirk to form on my face.

"The one that I plan on killing."

"He's not important because that's not my man. I don't think you should kill him, he doesn't deserve to die."

"You have feelings for that nigga?" my jaw tensed and my grip on her waist got tighter as I waited for her answer.

"No," she whispered, looking away from me.

"Don't turn away from me when you answering this question, Macy. Do you have feelings for that nigga?" My voice was stern as I looked at her intensely.

"No pa, I don't have feelings for him. I haven't had feelings for anyone since you," she said honestly.

"Yeah ight tell me anything," I told her.

"I'm serious Haze," she told me.

"Break Up" by Mario was playing and Gucci Mane's part was about to come up. I looked right into Macy eyes and could tell she was telling the truth, yet I still didn't want to believe her.

*"Now baby girl have dumped me, she no longer wants me. I'm no longer hired she says that I've been fired. On to the next one more fish in the sea. Girls are like buses miss one, next 15 one comin'. Haze crazy and his ice game stunnin' swag so stupid still you straight dumped me. Over, no more smokin' doja. Baby girl went AWOL, she used to be my soulja."* I rapped along with Gucci letting Macy know how I was feeling.

"I didn't dump you I had no choice but to leave. My father didn't want us to be together so he forced me to move to Philly. I wanted to reach out to you I really did, my father just made it damn near impossible. You don't have to question my love for you Haze because you always had it. The night I saw you at Geno's my heart began beating again. The night at your house I felt more alive than I did in the last two years."

"Then why did you chose your father Macy? I would've taken care of you, I would've made sure that you were straight no matter what. All you had to do was choose me and stay."

"I do choose you I've always chosen you. I choose you today and I'll continue to choose you over and over and over again. I will choose you without pause, without doubt and in a heartbeat. When it comes to any choice whether you are a part of my choices or not, you Haze Young will always be my first fucking choice."

She was crying as she was talking and my heart melted. Hearing her say she chose me opened up the gate where I locked my feelings away. I wiped her tears and pulled her into my chest. I didn't know what to say to her but I wasn't about to let her cry out in public like that.

"Stop crying Macy, I get it ma. I get it."

"No I don't think you do. I'm willing to do whatever it takes just to have you in my life again. Just to have you hold me in your arms and call me, ma. I plan on doing anything I need to do pa to prove my love to you."

Her tears had her eyes glossy as they continued to fall from her eyes. I couldn't take this shit anymore. I forced her mouth against mine kissing her with everything I had in me. I couldn't speak the words I knew she wanted to hear so this kiss was gonna have to tell her everything I couldn't.

I ended the kiss and the same thing that danced around in my eyes is the same thing that danced around in hers; lust.

"You scared to ride on the back of my bike?" I asked her.

"No why?"

"I want to get out of here and your coming with me. I've been craving you and now that I have you in front of me I'm not letting you go until I get what I want."

"Just don't hurt me," she said softly.

"I can't promise that I won't hurt you because what you want isn't something I can give you right now, Macy. This ain't me running game either. I need to feel you wrapped around me I just can't be there for you the way you want me to. I'm not saying it's going to be like this forever, it's just like this right now for the moment."

Everything I was saying to Macy right now was the truth. I needed her sex the way lungs need air. No one else could satisfy me sexually and it was because I had got a taste of the sweetest loving known to man.

"Haze, when I said I will fight for you as long as it takes I mean that. If I can only have you sexually then I'm willing to take that. Just don't kill me on the back of your bike." She giggled.

Getting on the bike she wrapped her arms around my waist tightly as I pulled off. I wouldn't say this was a step for Macy and I because I still couldn't tell her how I felt. I loved the fuck out of this girl, my pride just wouldn't allow me to be with her. I was sure this sexual relationship Macy and I were going to embark on was probably going to fuck things up for us even more than they already were. When I got to that road I would across it but right now the only thing I cared about was dipping into the sweet caramel that Macy had in between her thighs.

## *14: Zeke*

"You didn't have to hit him like that, Zeeky. I was already going to handle the situation," Emanii complained.

"The fuck did you think I was going to do when you brought that up in my presence. Emanii, you're my sister did you honestly think I was just going to be cool with you a nigga putting his hands on you?"

"He's not just some nigga; he is your friend, Ezekiel."

"That shit don't mean nothing. I refuse to allow any nigga to put his hands on you when I don't even put my hands on you. Drix being my nigga just means he should've known better than to raise his fucking hand to you."

"You don't have to get mad at me, all I'm trying to say is that I have it handled." She rolled her eyes at me and Eniko laughed a little.

"If you had that shit handled then you shouldn't have brought it up in my presence. The next time that nigga puts his hands on you he's dead and that's word to Esque. Eniko, I don't know what the fuck you laughin' for. I should fuck yo ass up."

"How are you going to go on and on about someone putting their hands on me yet you are talking about putting your hands on Eniko?"

"Manii, mind your business cause this don't got nothing to do with you. Eniko and I have unfinished business we need to handle." I grabbed a Eniko's hand and when she didn't snatch it away from me I was surprised.

"You're not about to take her away from me leaving me here alone, Zeeky," Emanii whined.

"Then you can come with us and I'll drop you off at home."

"You get on my nerves. Just let me get some food and walk around then Eniko and I will be ready to go."

"Manii, you go ahead towards the food table and I'll catch up with you in a second," Eniko told her.

"Whatever."

Manii rolled her eyes walking away leaving Eniko and I alone. She was looking good in her jean shorts that slightly hung off her waist, a black crop top, and jays. Her hair was in two braids going back. Earrings graced her ears and a necklace adorned her neck. She was fly and fine. Eniko had really grown up and I wanted to explore each one of her grown up curves.

"I thought you were going to text me the next day," she said shyly.

"You needed space to get your head together. I wasn't about to cloud that shit up more. I needed you to be in a clear mental space so you could understand me when I tell you that you and I are together."

"Ezekiel, you can't just demand that we be together."

"I can and I just did. Think this shit is a game if you want to, Eniko. I don't just go down lickin' everyone girl. You allowed me to taste you, which allowed me entrance into your heart. We're a fucking team, ma."

"Zeke, I'm not trying to be tied down not to men—"

"I'm not even 'bout to let you waste your breath trying to explain to me the reason we not together or how we can't be together. I've already claimed you; I can white Nike you and wife you if that's what you want, boo."

"White Nike me?" She giggled and pushed me away from her. "You really gonna take that corny ass line and try to flip it? Since when did you become a rapper?"

"I'll become whatever I need to just to have you. Stop playing like you ain't like that line tho. I think I might wife her.

You know powder blue Roca wear suit white Nike her." I reach out to her and pulled her closer to me.

"Don't touch me with yo corny self," she joked, swatting my hands away.

I tussled with her for a minute before getting her in my arms. "You had more than enough space these past two years. From this point on ain't no space, ma. It's a me and you thing."

"I don't know about the whole me and you thing. I came out here to find me a prospect." She smiled biting her bottom lip while looking around at the dudes who were near us.

"Eniko, don't play with me. I don't fight niggas over a female I end their lives. I got the heat on my hip and I don't mind clearing this shit out over you. So if that's what you want then do you cause I got more than a few clips that need emptying."

"Ezekiel, stop it I was just joking. I wasn't serious at all," she told me with worry in her eyes.

"The shit might be a game or a joke to you but to me the shit is serious. I don't like sharing, ma."

My face was cold and stern letting her know I was dead ass. Eniko was gonna have a lot to learn about ya boy. Things done changed, we matured and grew a little colder. We've seen death and brought death to others at a young age. That shit doesn't leave a good taste in your mouth, but when you live the life you learn how to deal with the bitter taste.

"I can't do this Zeke," she said, pushing away from me.

"You can't do wha—"

"Ezekiel! I can't fucking believe you! I knew it!"

"Eniko, hold up ma." I slowly jogged towards her while Lemon was still yelling following me.

"No Zeke, it was nice talking to you but that's as far as this is going to go. I can't do this with you, as bad as I want to I can't."

"Just tell me what the problem is and I'll fix it."

"How, when you can't even fix the problem known as Lemon," Eniko gestured with her head behind me. I turned around and Lemon was standing there putting all her weight on her left leg. Her hands were folded over her chest, her lips were screwed up and she looked at me like her whole life came crashing down.

I turned back towards Eniko and stared at her for a second. She could say she wasn't doing this shit all she wanted. Her ass ain't no have no choice. I reached out for her pulled her to my side and draped my arm over her shoulder. She laughed rolled her eyes then crossed her arms.

"Lemon, wassup?" I asked with a smile on my face even though I was annoyed by her presence.

"Don't wassup me like everything is cool between the two of us. How can you stand there and smile like I'm not standing here while you are hugged up on another bitch. The same bitch that had a stupid ass crush on you when we were in high school. The same bitch that was dating your best friend. Is that really what we are doing now?"

"Sour head keep whatever beef you have between him and you. I came here to enjoy myself, not to mess up my nails by beating your ass!" Eniko snapped.

"If I remember correctly I didn't address you therefore you don't address me. Talking about beating my ass, bitch you wish. Zeke, do you even have anything to say for yourself?"

"Lemon, what more do you want? I already told you that I was good on you yet you still feel the need to step to me when I'm trying to move on. I don't want you Lemon ight so let whatever fantasy you got of us being together go."

"You always say you're done and you come running right back. How do you expect me to take this any different?"

"I'ma take that because I'm not gonna embarrass your ass out here. I'm letting you know now there is never going to be an us again, ight.

"You could never embarrass me because I'm the one that could end your world. Now it's either you are going to be with me or you won't be around long enough to be with anyone else?"

I let go of Eniko and walked close to Lemon. I stretched my arms out as if I was going to give her a hug. She came into my arms with a smile on her face. I ran my fingers in her hair then grabbed a hand full and forced her head to the side.

"Lemon, if we weren't in a public place at a public event I would send one single bullet right through your heart. Don't fuckin' threaten my life again unless you are ready for yours to be over." I let her go and moved away from her as she cried out for me.

I ignored her ass, grabbed Eniko's hand, and walked away. Lemon could be heard in the distance screaming my name, but I paid her no mind. I was tired of the shit with Lemon, I could understand why she didn't want to believe we were over. Time and time again we would find our way back in each other's bed, but this time was different. The person I always wanted was back in my life and I refused to let anything fuck up what I was trying to do with Eniko. The both of us were still young so marriage wasn't even a thought in my mind. All I wanted was to be able to call her mine and to have her call me hers. Nothing major just that simple shit.

"Zeke, let me go because it's apparent you have a lot going on in your life right now."

"I don't have shit going on in my life, Eniko."

"You out here talking about killing people behind me, and you got Lemon damn near begging you to be with her. Then you are still out here in these streets doing the same shit that got Liam killed. I can't be around that shit Zeke," she said frustrated.

"What I do in the streets don't got nothing to do with you cause y'all not on the same level. I'm not going to say that I'm going to be alright because every time I step out the door I have a chance of dying. That shit ain't because I live the street life, it's because I live in the fucking hood. Whether I'm working a nine to five or hustling I can still walk out the door and get killed."

"You chances just increase because you are hustling, Zeke. I told myself a long time ago that I wasn't going to fuck with another hustler and I meant that, so tell me why should I give you a chance. Why should I risk getting my heart broken again? Why should I risk it all, Zeke?"

We were in the middle of the block arguing over something so fucking stupid. My jaw tensed as I watched her cry asking me why she should risk it all. I wasn't one of the public attention and that was exactly what we were receiving. Everyone who was on the block was staring at the two of us.

"I'm not gonna do this shit out here, Eniko. You wanna talk we can go get in my car and go back to the crib," I told her.

"No if you want me the way you say you do you will say whatever you need to say right now!" she yelled.

"Eniko, chill out and just go talk to him," Emanii said, coming to Eniko's side.

"No Emanii. Whatever he has to say he should be able to say it right here. Why doesn't he want to say something cause all these people are watching? These are his people right, he's the man in the streets, right. Then why the fuck can't he man up right now?"

"Hit me when you ready to talk in private. I'm not the type of nigga that keeps his business in the streets because he be in the streets." I walked off from Eniko not saying shit else to her.

I didn't have a problem confessing my feelings to Eniko I just wasn't going to do that shit with a fucking audience. I could have enemies I didn't know nothing about and they could've been watching. The first thing they would do to try and get at me was taking Eniko's ass. I wasn't going to risk her life cause she wanted a fucking public display of affection.

## 15: Eniko

Days passed and the whole ordeal with Zeke was still on my mind. I just couldn't understand for the life of me why he just couldn't tell me what he wanted from me. He wanted me to go against something I felt strongly about for him, yet he couldn't even give me a real reason why he was worth the risk worth the effort. Even though I was hung up on Zeke I didn't let that stop me from doing me. Gavin had called me the same night of the block party telling me he wanted me to come up to Philly and see him. Since I didn't have anything going on out in NY I jumped in my car and made my way to Philly. Before I linked up with Gavin I wanted to stop and see my mother.

Talking to her lately I've been hearing something different in her voice. She was usually cheerful and full of life whenever but that was no longer there. Her and Martin were supposed to be going to traveling, the only problem was Martin was doing most of the traveling on his own. I never really got into my mother's relationship with Martin because I have always felt it was none of my business. However, I refuse to sit around and allow my mother to be mistreated, especially when I knew she deserved so much better.

I pulled into the driveway parked my car and hoped out. Walking up to the front door, I used my key to let me myself in and all I heard playing was Mary J. Blige.

"ERINN!!!" I yelled, searching the house for my mother.

I kept yelling out her name until I made it up to her bedroom where the music was coming from. Her door was closed, she wasn't answering when I called her name, and a depressing song was playing, so all thoughts of knocking on her door went out the window. I busted through her door and go the shock of my life.

"ENIKO!!!"

"OH MY GOD, MOM!" My mother was upside down in the arms of a man I didn't recognize giving him head while he was eating her out.

She didn't even have to say anything else because once it full registered in my mind what was going on I rushed out her room and into the bathroom trying to throw water on my face to erase the images I just saw.

*Why would she be sexin' to that song out of all songs and where the hell is Martin?* I questioned myself. I couldn't bring myself to go anywhere but to my old bedroom. I sat on the bed waiting for my mother to come to me with an explanation because I damn sure wasn't going to come to her.

*Nickels for my thoughts, dimes in my bed. Quarters of the Kush, shape the liens in my head. Take my verses too serious ya hate me, cause I'm the one to paint a vivid picture no HD. Yeah. I want it all, that's why I strive for it. Diss me and you'll never hear a reply for it. Any awards show or party I'll get fly for it. I know what's coming I just hope I'm alive for it.*

Hearing Drake's song "Successful" blare from my phone caused me to put what I just saw my mother doing to the side and answer my phone.

"Hello."

"Where you at? I'm sitting on your bed and you ain't here." I rolled my eyes because Zeke was so extra.

"Why are you even in my house, Zeke? I haven't heard from you in days and now you want to do random pop up visits at my house?"

"Stop with all the questions and just tell me where you at."

"I'm in Philly visiting my mother."

"When do you get back?"

"I'm not sure when I'm coming back, but when I do I don't want to see you."

"You don't even believe that lie you just told yourself. Stop playing, when you touch down hit my line. Don't make me have to come find you cause that shit ain't gonna be pretty, Eniko."

"Whatev—" before I could even get my word Zeke hung up the phone.

I dialed Macy's number to find out why she thought it was okay to let Zeke in the house when I wasn't there. A part of me knew calling her was a waste of time because since the block party getting in touch with her was damn near impossible. She had been with Haze for the last couple of days ignoring everyone's calls and just doing her. Just like I thought Macy didn't answer the phone. I hung up and was going to leave the room to find my mother when she walked in my room first.

"Eniko, why would you just bust into my bedroom like that?" was the first thing out of her mouth.

"Ma, I walked in the house and the first thing I heard was "Not Gon' Cry". Then I started calling out your name and you didn't respond. What else was I supposed to do when I found out the music was coming from your room. The thought of you having sex never even crossed my mind. Why would you even have sex to that song, and who was the guy? Is everything okay with you and Martin? Ma, what is going on?"

"If you would slow down I will explain everything."

She grabbed a chair that I had in my room and sat on it. She crossed her legs and looked at me with tears in her eyes. I wanted to comfort her but I didn't know if she even needed comforting. I didn't know if she was crying because she had been hurt or because she got caught cheating.

"Things with Martin and I have been rough since April. For the most part, we hid our issues from you and Macy because the both of y'all were dealing with a lot. When y'all moved out three weeks ago things, started to get worse. We were supposed to be traveling yet most of the time he was going on trips by himself. Sometimes he would say that he was coming home late and wouldn't come home at all. Whenever I would ask him about it he would tell me that I didn't have anything to worry about.

How can I not worry though, Eniko? He is staying out all times of the night and going on trips alone. I asked him is there another woman and he assured me that their wasn't. His actions though, and I don't think he can even tell the difference. I have been played before by your father and I refuse to be played a second time. I'm not saying me sleeping with someone else in the same bed Martin and I share is the right thing to do but it's what makes me feel better at the moment. I've cried and had many sleepless nights and I refuse to have anymore. My heart is broken and my ego is bruised."

After my mother said all of that I didn't even know what to say. I was only eighteen and even though I experienced a lot at a young age I never experienced something like this. I didn't know where to begin to make my mother feel better.

"Wow! I'm shocked, I would've never guessed you and Martin would be having those types of problems."

"Me either, especially since we been friends for so long. I just don't know. Anyway, I should even be having this conversation with my eighteen-year-old daughter. What made you come to Philly?"

My mother wiped the tears from her eyes and forced a smile on her face. It hurt that I couldn't give her the type of advice I knew she would give me if I needed it. I wanted to be here for my mother I just didn't know how to be.

"I came out here because I'm supposed to be going on a date, and I wanted to check on you because lately I've noticed you sounding different on the phone."

"Don't worry about me, I'm going to be fine and everything will work it's self out. Who are you going on a date with?"

"Gavin. He's one of Rex's friends. He seems cool and we text and talk on the phone a lot we just never really been out by ourselves."

"Is that's why Macy isn't with you?"

"No Macy is back in New York doing her own thing," I said not giving away too much.

"Well you go ahead and go on your date. I'm happy you are starting to get back out there, just because you had one bad experience doesn't mean they are all going to be bad."

As soon as she said that I instantly thought about Zeke. I wanted to take that chance on Zeke, I really did. I was just scared of what the outcome may be if I did take that chance.

"It's funny that you say that. Before I started dating Liam, I had a little crush on Emanii's brother Zeke. I've ran into him a couple of times since I've been back in New York. He wants to date and I want to date him I'm just a little hesitant because of his lifestyle. How things ended with Liam has me scared that things with Zeke is going to end up the same way."

"First let me say that I can't tell you who you can and can't date but what I am going to tell you is that being a girlfriend to someone who runs the streets isn't an easy thing nor is it a thing I want for you. You deserve so much more than to be a thug's girlfriend or a dope boy's wife."

"I know I deserve more than that. It's just that the feeling I get when I'm around him is one that stays with me even days after I seen him. He causes me to melt without even trying. I know he isn't the type of guy I need in my life, but he makes it hard not to want to be with him. I honestly thought after all this time my feelings for him would fade away but they haven't and that has to count for something." I sighed.

"Yeah they count for something and that's exactly why I refuse to tell you who you can and can't date. You're eighteen now and this is the time where you are going to make mistakes and date the wrong person. You may even date two people at once and that's okay too. Most importantly, at this age you will act on certain things because of your feelings. Your feelings play a big part in your decision making and they will cause you to make bad choices and good choices. It's up to you to figure out which are which, Eniko. Your feelings for Zeke are strong so you say. The only way you are going to find out if what you are feeling is the real deal is to give him a chance. This is where your maturity level will come into play. Even though you are acting on your feelings it's going to take your level of maturity to get you through the bad times and trust me there are going to be bad times. He is going to get you upset and you are gonna fight over him but it's going to be your maturity not your feelings that help you decided if the bad times are worth the good times with him."

"I don't want to fight over him, Ma. How does that look me in the streets fighting another chick over something that is supposed to be mine? Have you ever done that?"

"I'm not saying that you fighting over him is going to look good because it's not. It's going to tear you down after a while but it's something you're gonna do if the love you have for him is as strong and as real as you say your feelings for him are. When the love is real woman refuses to let another woman come in and try to steal what's hers. Real love causes woman to make a fool of themselves over the ones they love."

"I don't want to be in love if I'm ever going to make a fool of myself. When I was with Liam I never made a fool of myself and I refuse to do it with anyone else."

"Eniko, when you were in love with Liam things were different, you were fifteen. You're eighteen now and the way you view love has changed. You're taking what I'm saying as if I'm telling you that you are going to embarrasses yourself behind a person you love when that's not what I'm saying at all. What I'm saying is that love will have you doing things that you say you would never do. You can sit here and tell me that if a chick was all over your man you wouldn't fight her but let love bite you in the ass and you find yourself in that scenario; I will bet my last dollar you would fight that chick because that's what love does for woman. Love will have a woman crying over her man all the while beating his ass.

We as woman think love does a number on us but the way love effects a man doesn't even compare. A man that is in love will risk it all for the woman he loves. He will throw his life away just so she could have hers if he needed to. Love effects woman emotionally while love effects men mentally."

I listened to my mother talk and everything she was saying had me scared to even say those three words. I didn't want to be an emotional wreck all because I fell in love.

"Listen Eniko, love is a beautiful thing and I don't want you to be scared of experiencing it because of the things I said. Everything I said is the truth but it's not every woman's truth."

"I know Ma and thank you for talking to me."

"That's what I'm here for baby. Now go ahead on your date and enjoy your time. Before you leave come back to the house and we can have dinner together."

"We can have dinner tonight if you want to. I really don't want to leave you alone," I told her.

"It's fine, Eniko. I'm a big girl and what Martin and I are going through is something that we are gonna have to work out. I don't want you stressing over it because it's not for you to stress over. Also, don't bring it up to Macy what you saw here today, just keep it to yourself."

"Oh trust me I'm not bringing it up to Macy."

"Okay good and the next time you speak to Emanii tell her I said hello."

"I will." My mother and I hugged each other then she walked me to the door.

I got in my car pulling off to go meet Gavin. I was going to use this date with Gavin to forget what I caught my mom doing and just to forget about everything in general. I didn't want to think about the conversation my mother and I just had and I didn't want to think about Zeke. All I wanted to do was enjoy my time without thinking too much into the situation.

It took an hour to get to Gavin's house. I remained in my car texting Gavin and letting him now I was outside. Whenever I went to a neighborhood I wasn't used to I would tell whoever I was meeting to come and get me from the car.

"You could've got out the car wasn't nothing going to happen to you out here," Gavin said, opening my car door.

I stepped out giving him a hug and as his arms wrapped around me, Zeke's words replayed in my head. *I don't fight niggas over a female I end their lives.* I quickly ended the hug and took a couple of steps back from him. When Zeke said it you couldn't help but to take him seriously because his voice was laced with menace.

"You ight, Eniko?" Gavin asked, looking at me sideways.

"Uh yeah I'm fine." I shook off the cold chill that ran through my body and forced a smile on my face.

"I don't know what's up with you. Every time we text or talk on the phone you cool as shit. Whenever I get yo ass in person you wanna act like you scared of a nigga or something," he told me, taking my hand and leading me in the house.

"Scared of who, you? Please Gavin, you wouldn't hurt a fly let alone hurt me," I told him laughing.

"I would fuck a fly up cause them shits annoying as fuck. As for you the only hurting I plan on doing to you is also going to bring you pleasure. That's some shit you don't know nothing about nor are you ready for."

"What makes you think I'm not ready?" I asked just playing along.

"The look of nervousness in your eyes whenever I touch you. When I kiss you I light up your eyes but as my hands travel my body that light fades away and nervousness replaces it. I'm not trippin' tho cause what I got to offer is going to have you fucked up in the head anyway. I would rather make sure we're a team before puttin' this dick in yo life."

"I doubt your lil' package could have my head fucked up," I sassed, walking through his house. His décor from what I could see was well put together. He had a black, olive green and gold color scheme going on in his living room and kitchen. I was impressed because usually dudes didn't put much thought into what their house looked like. Gavin had a pretty olive green L shaped couch with gold accents and throw pillows on it. His entertainment system was black marble along with his coffee table.

"I don't know what nigga you referring to when you say lil' package cause ain't shit little about mine." He pulled down his basketball shorts exposing himself and little wasn't the right word to describe him at all. Although he wasn't extra-long, the thickness of his penis had my wondering what it taste like. A couple of veins were visible making it look even more perfect.

"It's beautiful," I mumbled still looking at it. Hearing him laughed made realize that I called his penis beautiful aloud.

"I mean it's alright looking," I said, trying to save face.

"Nah you got it right the first time my shit is beautiful. Like I said earlier though you not ready for the pain and pleasure my man brings. You can make yourself at home in the living room. You hungry?"

"Yeah, but not for any burnt or poisonous food."

"I see you got jokes. Don't play yo self ma, my moms taught me well."

"You can't be serious. You can really cook?"

"Bring yo ass in the kitchen so I can show you what I'm working with."

For the next hour and a half I watched Gavin move around the kitchen all the while making idle chit chat with him. A lot of our conversation went through one ear and out the other because I had other things on my mind. Watching Gavin cook turned me on in the worse way. I didn't know why it had such an effect on me but it did. He was good looking, his package was right, and he could cook, I was ready to hand my heart over to him on a silver platter. Gavin seemed like the whole package and if I was ready to settle down he would definitely be the one for me. I was starting to have second thoughts about dating both Zeke and Gavin. I had history with one and the other one seemed like Mr. Perfect. I wasn't sure what I was going to do I was just glad I didn't have to make the choice right now.

## *16: Macy*

"Macy I'm not playin' with yo ass. Tell that nigga you done with him. I'm trying to be nice about the situation but you pushing the shit. I already owe that nigga a couple of bullets. He gonna end up claiming them shits if I have to tell him for you," Haze threatened. He kissed me on the forehead then rolled out of bed as if what he just said was normal.

For the past four days Haze and I have been getting reacquainted with each other or should I say we were getting reacquainted with each other's bodies. Our days consisted of Haze going out to handle business, me staying in the house sleeping the day away, and making sure he had a meal on the table when he came home. Dessert always consisted of the two of us having the most beautiful, nasty, sinful sex that two people could have. Nothing was off limits when it came to our bedroom activities.

"When you going to meet with that nigga to tell him you done?" Haze asked, coming back in the room. I lustfully stared at his body, he was standing in front of me wearing nothing put a pair of polo briefs. His muscular build was hard to miss and the tattoos that adorn his skin didn't do nothing but cause my juices to flow. I reached in between my legs and started rubbing myself as I stared into his cold eyes. This thug persona he had going on was a turn on and I couldn't get enough of it.

"Macy, move your fuckin' hand man," he said, licking his lips.

"If I remove my hand what are you going to replace it with?" I smirked.

"I'm trying to talk to you bout some serious shit. A nigga gonna catch a body behind yo ass and all you can think about is getting a nut off."

"I can't help that I'm addicted. Just let me get a little bit then you can have my undivided attention."

"Lay back and lift them legs up."

I did as he said and prepared myself for whatever he was about to give me. He slipped in between my legs pressing his dick against my clit. A shiver came over me as he placed soft kisses against my neck. I went to wrap my arms around him but he forcefully pushed them into the bed.

"Don't touch me unless I tell you to."

"Okay," I whispered.

His lips found mine and that's when the euphoric feeling came over me. He was biting and sucking on my lips and snaking his tongue in and out of my mouth at the same time. His kiss left my mouth, traveled down to my chest until they found my nipples. He was kissing my nipples barely touching them. The light cool breeze of his breath against my nipples drove me crazy. I reached out of his head trying to force my nipple into his mouth.

"Chill the fuck out before I leave you here horny and wet. I said don't touch me until I tell you to." Once again he roughly took my hands and forced them on the bed. With his hands still holding mine his teeth gripped my nipple causing me to yelp out in pain.

"That's what you wanted, right? You wanted your nipple in my mouth so take that shit."

Haze didn't ease up on my nipple at all. He kept biting it and tugging on it roughly. The pain eventually turned into pleasure and when it did he went all out sucking and licking my nipple.

"Hazzzzze!" I cried out in pure bliss.

If I wasn't turned on before I was turned on now. The way his tongue flicked across each nipple had my legs shaking. I was ready to erupt and if Haze kept going at my nipples the way he did I was going to release like a volcano.

"Don't come yet," he told me.

"I can't hold it Haze. I don't know what you are doing to my nipples but that shit is driving me crazy."

"I need you to hold it Macy. I need you to hold it until I get down there. Promise you gonna hold it."

"I can't Haze."

"I said fuckin' promise me, Macy. You let that shit go you won't be getting any sex for a week."

"A week, Haze?" I panicked.

"A week. Hold it."

He went back to kissing all around my breasts and down my stomach. His hands sunk into my things driving me crazy. The more his lips touched my skin the more my body wanted to exploded. I bite into my bottom lip trying not to let any moans escape.

Haze took his time when he got to my stomach. His tongue swirled around my belly button a couple times. When he brought his face to my pussy I sighed a breath of relief. I was ready to let everything I had go but Haze didn't want me there yet. He completely passed my spot and went to sucking on my inner thighs. The nipple action he was showing me before had nothing on what he was doing to my thighs. The way he was sucking on them had me move from the left to the right. I had to resist from holding his head still and throwing my pussy into his face.

His hands gripped my thighs as my legs went on his shoulders and a smile spread across my face. I closed my eyes because I was about to get what I wanted.

"Macy," he called out.

"What Haze." I sighed. All I wanted was for him to give me that tongue action then we could go on about our business.

"I need you to hold out until I get to Z," he said with the most serious expression I ever seen.

"What you mean Z?" I asked confused.

"Just hold out until Z, ight."

He winked at me and before I could even try to figure out what he was talking about I felt his tongue against my clit. He wasn't moving his tongue in a regular way it felt like he was spelling out the alphabet against my slit.

"OH MY GOD HAZE!!!!" I cried out in pleasure when he formed the letter O.

"Remember Z, you can hold my head if you have to just make sure you wait for Z," he groaned.

I gripped his head trying my hardest to throw it all in his face. By the time he got to V my whole body was shaking uncontrollably. I only had four letters left and I didn't think I was going to make it.

"Haze I'm about to... I'm about to—"

"You ain't about to do shit until I form this Z," he whispered.

His tongue started from side of one of my lips came across my clit to the other lip, he then went diagonal and by the time he ended the Z at my opening my juices were pouring out of me.

"YESSSSSSSSSSSSSSSSSSSSSSS!" I cried out. The tears were streaming down my face faster than I was able to wipe them. The orgasm I just experience was one that I would never be able to describe.

Haze laid his body on top of mine and looked me in the eyes. He laughed as he wiped the tears away and all I could do was smile as the tears kept coming.

"That shit was powerful, huh?"

"Nigga you made me cry doing that shit you just did. You know you mine now right," I told him.

"What you—"

"All I need you to say is that you understand what I mean when you say your mine. We don't have to put a label on shit right now. We can go the speed you want to go. All I'm saying is that I don't want you doing what you do to me to anyone else. What you just did is liable to have me sitting in a jail cell if I catch you with another female."

"The fuck you think is going to happen with ole boy when I catch up to him? End shit with him Macy and I'm serious. I'm not ready to take things there with you on a relationship tip but as far as sexin' goes don't nobody touch what's mine."

"And no one touches what's mine."

"Now that we on the same page go handle your business and make sure you come back here when you finish."

"I'll think about it," I told him. I pushed him off of me then stepped out the bed ready to shower then handle my business.

"Don't play with me, Macy. I'll fuck yo little ass up then kill that nigga."

"And you don't play with me Haze. I don't want no shit when it comes to you and these bitches."

I walked out his room before he could say anything else because there honestly wasn't nothing else for him to say. The same way Haze didn't want me fucking with anyone was exactly how I felt when it came to him. We didn't have to be together for us to be together. It was going to take time for us to become a couple and I was okay with that. What I wasn't going to tolerate was him having a gang of bitches. I refused to allow Haze to do what he did to me to other chicks. I was gonna be the only one shedding tears behind his tongue and stroke game.

\* \* \*

I bite my nails waiting for Rex to text me and say that he was here. Little did Haze know while he was out handling business I hit Rex up letting him know that we needed to talk this weekend. He told me that he would come up here on Friday. I don't know if Haze looked through my text messages but I found it funny today out of all days would be the day Haze brought up Rex. I didn't have deep feelings for Rex, but I also didn't want to see him dead. From the way Haze moved I knew he wasn't joking when he said he would kill Rex. Haze had turned into a straight savage and I wasn't going to call his bluff. Right after I told Rex that what we had was over, I planned on going back over to Haze's place cook him and dinner then fuck him silly.

I was trying to get in as much sex as I could because when school started Haze and I weren't going to be able to spend that much time with each. I wanted to make sure he got enough of my good good so then he would understand that no one could do him the way I do him. I already knew that no one could do me the way Haze did, which was why I didn't take any dude too serious. Rex somehow became the exception and now things had to end. It was cool while it lasted but I had my savage again and nothing was better than what he had to offer.

My phone vibrating on my kitchen counter caught my attention. I rushed over to it and read the text from Rex telling he was downstairs. For a split second I thought about whether I should allow him upstairs or talk to him outside. Outside might have been too public and I didn't want to bring him up here either because Eniko was in her room sleeping. I grabbed my keys off the counter and ran out the door. I figured we could talk in my old house, which was downstairs.

"Wassup ma, you lookin' good," Rex said, pulling me into a hug when I opened the door for him. I hugged him back but when his hands went down to my ass I cut the hug short.

"Come on so we can talk, Rex." I lead him into my old apartment then closed the door behind me.

"Why you actin' like you don't know me and shit?" he asked, looking at me suspiciously.

"Rex this thing between us isn't going to work. You live in Philly and I live out here. I'll be starting school at the end of August and I won't have much time to see you."

"That's straight bullshit and you know it, Macy. Whatever you trying to say, say the shit cause this bullshit ass excuse you're trying to sell me I'm not buying."

"I'm not selling you a bullshit excuse I'm telling you the truth. I hardly see you or hear from you know. It's only going to get worse when I'm a full time student."

"Yeah ight Macy, you can feed me that bullshit all you want. I'm not leavin' out of here until you keep it a buck with me."

"What do you mean you're not leavin' until I keep it a buck with you? Come on Rex don't do this because we are better than that."

"Nah, we not better than that because you sitting up here lying in my face and shit. You really trying to insult my intelligence and I'm not feeling that shit."

"I'm not trying to insult anything. If you don't want to take what I'm saying as the truth then that's on you. What I'm not going to do is sit here with you like I don't have stuff to do."

"What you got to do, go back to that fuck nigga's house?"

"What?" I asked shocked.

"You heard what the fuck I said. You really think I don't know what you been up to and why you haven't been answering my calls and shit? Macy I'ma street nigga so I watch my investments, ma. You didn't think I was just going to let my girl move to another state without me keeping tabs on her did you?"

"You've been following me?" I asked nervously.

"I'm too busy of a nigga to be following you Macy, but I have been keeping tabs on you. I don't appreciate you fucking with that nigga tho. I'm gonna need you to stop fucking with ole boy."

"Rex, I don't know where you get off thinkin' you can tell me what to do but I only have one daddy and he ain't you. Now again I have stuff I have to do and I'm going to need you to leave."

"I'm not leaving here until you call that nigga up and let him know that you don't want shit to do with him."

"I'm not doing—"

"MACY, OPEN THIS FUCKING DOOR BEFORE I KICK THE SHIT DOWN!"

*Do this nigga got a GPS planted inside of me or some shit. How the fuck did he know I was here?* I said to myself.

"You heard that man Macy, go and open the door." Rex smirked.

I was starting to feel like these niggas were setting me up or some shit. I was only about five steps away from the door but those five steps seemed like the longest five steps of my life. I swung the door open and was immediately knocked down to the ground. Haze and Zeke both stormed in with guns in their hands

"Nigga, didn't yo mother ever tell you to not touch what doesn't belong to you?" Haze gritted.

"Fellas what's with the guns? Things are not even that serious." Rex laughed as if he wasn't about to die right here.

"Nigga, it is that serious when you were touching what belongs to me. I don't fucking share, this shit ain't kindergarten."

"What you want to do with this nigga?" Zeke asked Haze.

"I don't know I'm in a good mood and shit. Should I let this nigga make it?"

"The question shouldn't be if you should let me make it the questions should be if I should let you make it? Unless you want to leave out of this place in pieces I suggest you allow me to walk out of this door alive."

"Nigga, you talking big shit for someone who has two guns pointed at him!" Zeke spat.

"And you talking big shit for someone who has numerous red dots on their bodies," Rex laughed. "Like I said unless you want you want to leave out of here in pieces I suggest you allow me to walk out of here alive."

"Haze, just let him go," I cried still on the floor. I wasn't sure what Rex had a planned or if he had anything planned at all. All I knew as that I saw red dots on both Zeke and Haze and I wasn't about to lose them.

"You must've been in a saint in your past life because once again you have been touched by an angel. You know what they say about a nigga who keeps cheatin' death, right?" Haze smirked, lowering his gun.

"Touché," Rex smiled. He walked towards the door but stop to look at me before he walked out. "I'll be in touch, make sure you answer the phone when I call." He winked at me then left out.

Haze slammed the door after that nigga then glared at me as if I was his worst enemy.

"The fuck is that about, Macy?" he asked me.

"I don't know Haze I'm just as clueless as you. Before the two of y'all came in he was talking to me as if he had someone watching me or something."

"FUCK!" Haze yelled, punching the wall. My ass stayed on the floor because I was too afraid to move. I didn't know what was going and I was too scared to ask.

"Nigga, chill the fuck out. You punching walls and shit isn't going to help nothing. Macy get up, ma." Zeke helped me off the floor then stood next to me while all I could do was look at Haze.

"What type of shit is that nigga involved in, Macy?"

"I don't know Haze. I know he hustles but that's it," I told him honestly.

"We need to find out who that nigga is and quick. We also need to hold a meeting between the family. We all got to move and get new rides," Zeke said.

"I'ma go dump Macy's car then take her to get a room or some shit cause we can't go back to the crib."

"Why can't we go back to the crib?" I asked

"That nigga knows more about us then he cares to let on. The fact he had niggas in range to kill us shows that he ain't no average street nigga. I don't want you getting caught up in the cross fire," Haze told me.

"Where's Eniko at?" Zeke asked me.

"She's upstairs sleep."

"I'm going to take her back to my crib. We will have a meeting in the morning."

"Ight my nigga, be safe." Haze and Zeke dapped each other up before Haze grabbed my hand and lead me out the house.

We walked right past his car and started walking up the block. "Why aren't we getting in the car?"

"I don't trust that nigga and I don't know what the fuck he might've had his people do to our cars."

"But you just said you wanted to dump my car."

"You right, damn." He laughed a little.

"Are you mad at me?" It was stupid question to ask but I needed to know. We were on speaking terms and I was praying like hell that what happened didn't mess up what we had going on.

"How can I be mad at you Macy? From the way yo ass stayed on the ground I knew you didn't know what the hell was going on. I'ma have to take you to the gun range or something because I can't have yo ass getting caught up and crying on the floor."

"Shut up Haze, it's not funny." I was glad he was making light of the situation because him being mad at me was something I wouldn't have been able to take.

"Nah seriously though, things are going to get real and I can't have anything happening to you Macy. I love you ma and I'll die before I allow you to get hurt."

Hearing him say he loved me caused me to stop walking. I stood there as Haze turned around and looked at me. "Why you stop walking, ma? We need to get back to your car so we can dump it and get a room."

"Haze, do you really love me?" I asked like I was school girl waiting for my crush to pass me a note back letting me know if he liked me or not.

"Macy, do we have to do this shit right now?"

"I know now might not be the right time to have this conversation but I have to know. I need to know what you just said to me was the truth. I don't know if tomorrow is going to be promised to me so this is something that I need to know now."

"Shut the fuck up with that you don't know if tomorrow is promised shit. That Rex nigga isn't going to hurt you, and I put that on my momma. As for me loving you that shit never changed, you hurt a nigga on some real shit but never caused my love for you to stray. If I didn't love yo ass anymore best believe I wouldn't have fucked you or kept you at my house for the past four days. Even after all these years my heart still beats for yo big headed ass."

"I love you too, Haze!" I cried as I leaned up to kiss him and let him know that I meant what I said. He kissed me back with so much passion I almost stripped out of my clothes in the middle of the block and gave him all of me so he knew it was real.

"Chill the fuck out before I take your shit right here in broad daylight."

"I wouldn't even be mad at you if you did that shit, daddy," I purred.

"You fucking reckless ma and I love that shit."

"So does this mean we are together?" We were still hugged up in the middle of the block as if my ex didn't tell me that he has been watching me and as if Haze didn't almost die.

"We don't need titles ma, just let it be what it's going to be."

"Okay." I dropped the conversation because I didn't want to push things.

He grabbed my hand and lead me back to my car. I tossed him my keys and we jumped in and drove off. He had told me that he loved me and that was good enough for me. Sooner or later we were going to revisit this conversation because something was telling me that he was holding back from me.

## 17: Zeke

"Eniko, wake up ma."

I sat at the edge of the bed shaking Eniko trying to wake her up. I haven't seen much of her since she came back from Philly. I had something special planned for her back at my crib, which was why I didn't mind taking that ride with Haze over here. If he would've told me that we were going to fuck up a conversation between Macy and her dude I would've been more prepared to have red fucking dots on my body. That shit came to a surprise to me. I didn't know who that nigga was but I could tell he was going to be problem. Solving problems wasn't nothing to us and this Rex nigga was going to be history soon enough.

"Gavin," Eniko mumbled, trying to rub the sleep out of her eyes. My jaw flexed from hearing another dude's name come out her mouth. That nigga was going to end up just like his fucking friend; dead.

"Eniko, open your eyes ma," I told her.

She sat up finished wiping the sleep out of her eyes then looked at me with a shocked expression." Zeke, what are you doing here?"

"I came to take you out. You been ducking me since you came back from Philly and I just wanted to do something nice for you."

"I haven't been ducking you, I've just been busy."

"Busy doing what? Chilling with my sister. You don't have to lie to me, Eniko."

"I'm not lying." She sighed.

"Try not to sigh too hard your breath is kicking," I joked.

"Shut up my breath does not stink." She brought her hand to her mouth licked it then smelled it.

"The fuck is you doing?" I asked her. That was the strangest shit I had ever seen.

"I'm trying to smell my breath. Shut up Zeke and get out."

"I'll get out of bed if you promise to never do that shit again."

"I'll make that promise. Now get out so I can go back to sleep."

"I know you heard me when I said I came here to take you out."

"I'm tired Zeke. I swear I caught your sister's pregnancy symptoms. All I want to do is eat and sleep." Eniko yawned then looked at me with those big bright eyes that I loved.

Everything about Eniko was perfect to me. From her big beautiful eyes all the way down to how she scrunched up her nose when she didn't like how something smelled. She was perfect and her ass was perfect for me.

"I promise you it's gonna be worth it and if it's not worth it I'll buy you whatever you want."

"I'm not fourteen anymore Zeke, the things I like are expensive."

"I'm not that broke sixteen-year-old anymore either. I got money ma whatever your heart desires is at my command."

"Fine, I'll go with you and if I don't have fun you have to buy my school books."

"School books that's it?"

"They not as cheap as you think they are." She smiled.

"Ight, that's a bet. Give me a kiss."

"Didn't you say my breath smelt bad, why would you want to kiss me?"

"I don't care how bad your breath smells I'ma always wanna kiss you. No matter how you smell or what you look like, you will always be beautiful to me."

"You laying it on thick, huh player?" she laughed.

"I'm not laying on nothing I'm just being honest with you. You have always been perfect to me and even though some time has passed, nothing has changed. You perfect in my eyes, ma."

"Thank you, Zeke."

She leaned over giving me a light kiss then pulled away. I wasn't having that shit though, I placed her my hand on her hips bringing her closer to me.

"Zeke, what are you doing?"

"Shhhhh," I whispered.

I pressed my lips against her and brought my hand between her legs.

"No Zeke," she managed to say in between us kissing.

"Chill out I'm not even trying to take it there with you. I'm just trying to see if you could get wet by a nigga just kissin' yo ass. From what I just felt yo ass is leaking."

"Shut up Zeke! Oh my god!" she covered her face as if she was embarrassed.

"Don't ever cover your face when you're with me. When it comes to me and you there isn't shit for you to be embarrassed about, ight." I removed her hands from her face and her skin was flushed red.

"Man, hurry up and get dressed before I give you something to be embarrassed about. Wear something comfortable too." I kissed her on the forehead then got off the bed. I was about to walk out the bedroom when she stopped me.

"Zeke wait," she said.

"Wassup?"

"Thank you for accepting me for who I am." She smiled getting out of the bed.

She walked up to me and placed one arm around my neck while the other rested at my crotch. She leaned up forcing her lips against mine. I slipped my hands into the boy shorts she had on while she caressed my lil' solider. Right before I could slip my hands to the front of her shorts, she pulled away from me.

"Why you fuckin' with me?" I asked her.

"I just wanted to see if I could get you hard from a kiss. From the way your solider is saluting me I can say that I did my job."

"So let me thank you for doing a job well done."

"No thanks is needed. I'm not even sure I like you let alone if I want to have sex with you."

"Stop lying ma that shit ain't cute. You feeling me and you know it. It's cute that you wanna play coy and all. I don't mind putting in the work because when it's all said and done you gonna be mine. Now get dressed before I leave yo big headed ass here."

I left out her room leaving her in there to get ready. Going in the living room I sat on the couch and waited for her. I wanted to make sure that Eniko had a good time tonight because come tomorrow things might not be so sweet. I didn't know who these niggas were that Macy and Eniko were fucking with, but I knew they weren't the average niggas. A part of me wanted to keep the whole situation away from Eniko because I didn't want her spazzing out. Telling her what was gonna go down wasn't doing nothing but setting myself up for a lecture. I wasn't trying to have another talk about how I could end up dead or any of that shit. I knew when she said things like that she was only trying to have my best interest at heart but the shit was depressing as fuck. Being in the streets I already knew that there was possibility of me dying, I didn't need the love of my life throwing that shit in my face too. Nine times out of ten I was going to keep her ass in the dark. The less she knew the better and the easier I would be able to handle things.

"The fuck is that?" I questioned standing up. I searched the couch looking for what was causing the vibration noise. Reaching in between the cushion I pulled out a phone. A whole bunch of texts popped up on the screen from that nigga Gavin. I slipped Eniko's phone in my pocket then went back to her bedroom.

"Aye what's the password to your phone?"

"Why?"

"I need to make a call. I left my phone in the car," I lied.

"0514"

"Ight and hurry up you taking forever and shit."

Going back in the living I unlocked her phone and dialed this nigga's number.

"You didn't have to call me you could've just sent a text back telling me what you wanted to do."

"Telling a nigga I plan on deading him is a little too explicit for text don't you think," I gritted.

"This must be the infamous Zeke."

"And you must be the dead nigga walkin'. Stop texting my girl."

"Nigga, I don't know how much of your girl she is cause the way she was actin' out here made it very believable that she was single."

"I don't give a fuck how she was making it seem, I'm tellin' you what it is. Stay away from my shawty man. I'm not about the back and forth just take heed to what the fuck I'm saying." I hung up the phone and slipped it into my pocket.

Eniko would eventually get her phone back, it just wasn't going to be no time soon. I needed Eniko's full attention to show her, it was meant to be between the two of us. She wanted to act like the lifestyle I lived was the reason we couldn't be together when in actuality it was because she was scared. Tonight though I wasn't taking no for an answer.

* * *

"Zeke, you did not do all of this?" she said with a shocked expression on her face.

Standing in the middle of the living room I had the whole front of my house lit dimly from the hues of the candles I placed all around the room. Pink and white rose petals were scattered all around and Maxwell's song "Pretty Wings" was playing softly in the background. I didn't know much about this romantic shit, but for Eniko I was willing to go above and beyond.

"If I didn't do it who else was going to do it? I just don't give anyone keys to my house."

"I don't even know what to say."

"Say you don't mind spending the rest of your life with me." I grabbed her and pulled her into my arms. I needed her to know that I was serious about the two of us being together. A nigga couldn't stress enough how much I needed her in my life.

"Ezekiel, I can't marry you. We haven't even dated or anything like that. Not to mention I'm only eighteen years old. Zeke we are way too young to get married."

"Slow up I'm not asking you to marry me. I don't even know you really, the feelings I have for you still stem off the person you were at fourteen years old. I don't even know if I'm still going to like you a year into us dating."

"Then why would you ask me to spend the rest of my life with you?"

"Cause I want you in my life whether we are friends or dating. I can't see my life without having you in it. I went two years without having you in it and that's not something I want to experience again. Things wasn't bad or nothing like that I just felt like a piece of me was missing. I didn't really realize that piece was you until yo ass came back."

"Zeke, you're confusing me, do you want to be my friend or do you want to be more than that? It's like one minute you are trying to get at me and then in the next you're afraid to express how you feel."

"Everything I'm saying to you and everything I've been saying to you is the truth. I want you as my friend and so much more Eniko. I'ma selfish nigga so if you gonna fuck with me then I have to be the only nigga in your life. I don't want you dealing with no dudes outside of the ones I call my brothers. So that nigga you been calling, texting, and spending time with has to go."

"I'm not sure who you are talking about." She was trying to play dumb like I didn't know another nigga was occupying her time.

"We not about to play that game because I played enough games and I'm done with that shit. I already told the nigga to stop calling you anyway, so the only thing left for you to do is change yo number."

"I'm not changing my number, Zeke. I'm not even sure if being with you is what I want to do."

"If you didn't want to be with me you wouldn't be here with me right now. You're not someone who does something she doesn't want to do. You here because you want to be wherever I'm at. It's okay you can admit it ma cause wherever you go you can bet your bottom dollar my ass will be right there with you."

"You really want to be with me," she said, looking at me shyly.

"I wouldn't be going through all this trouble if I didn't already see you as mine. I fucked up and let you get away before, but that shit's not happening twice."

"I'm yours," she said just above a whispered.

"Say word Eniko say word, ma." I smiled.

"I'm yours. Everything you said is the same exact way that I've been feeling. When I saw you in Geno's my feelings for you came rushing back. Just don't hurt me Zeke cause I can't handle it a second time."

"I would never hurt you intentionally. Hurting you is like hurting myself and I don't care too much for self-inflicting pain."

"Okay." The way she said it I could tell she was kind of unsure of her decisions. I brought her lips to mine kissing away any doubt she had.

"Slow down player you not getting none of this any time soon. You are on a probation period."

"Get the fuck out of here. My tongue and your clit are already well acquainted."

"And that shouldn't have happened. I'm serious Zeke we need to get to know each other again and I don't want sex to cloud our better judgement."

"Oh so you saying my dick gonna have you fucked up in the head, huh?" I joked.

"That's not what I'm saying. All I'm saying is that tasting this kitty and feeling it are two different things. My kitty is in an exclusive league all its own."

"What you saying, I'm not daddyish enough to get accepted into the exclusive club?"

"That's not what I'm saying at all, what I'm saying is I'm not easy and a cute little set up in the living room isn't going to open my legs for you."

"What if I said I had a set up in the bedroom as well that consisted of dozens of pink and white roses around the room, some more candles, and food?"

"That's sound nice but that still doesn't give you access. I would like my dinner in bed though."

"Third door on the left." She leaned up kissed me on the check then headed for the bedroom.

I wasn't even mad at Eniko for the way she just played me. She agreed to be mine with little to no effort and for that I was going to play this probation game with her. I wasn't sure how long it was going to last because I had needs that I only wanted her to fulfill. Going in the kitchen I pulled out the roast from the oven and sat it on the stove. I paid Emanii to cook dinner for Eniko and I because there was a lot of shit I could do, but cooking wasn't one of the things.

I pulled two plates from out of my cabinet and started making our plates. Emanii did her thing and I couldn't wait to dig in. She cooked a roast with carrots and potatoes, the sides consisted of white rice, black eyed peas and corn bread. I was gonna have to slip another hundred because she really did he thing. I placed Eniko's food and drink on a tray, and headed for the bedroom.

"Why you just standing there like that?" I asked her right before I stepped into the room. She was standing there frozen with the remote control in here hand. When I stepped into the room that's when I saw what she was looking at. On my TV was Liam getting shot and falling to the ground over and over again.

I sat the food down on the night stand then snatched the remote out her hand turning the TV off.

"Eniko, come here ma," I told her.

"Don't fucking touch me Zeke! Is this what you thought a romantic night is? How could you fucking do this to me!" She was yelling at the top of her lungs but that didn't stop her from crying.

"I didn't do this Eniko, I swear on my brother I didn't do this shit."

"Well who did because you just don't give your key to anyone!" She was looking at me with hurt and pain in her eyes. I felt like shit as she used my own words against me.

"I don't know who did this, Eniko." I tried to grab her again and this time she swung on me. I didn't even bother dodge the punch because I felt I deserved it. Her fist knocked with my right cheek and I just stood there and took it.

"I have to get out of here!" she sobbed.

"No you're not going nowhere." I told her. "You can't run as soon as a problem comes up, Eniko. We just got together if you run now you are always going to run when things pop up."

"This isn't something that just popped up, Zeke. Someone did this shit on purpose. Do you know how it made me feel to see Liam's body fall to the ground over and over again? I watched him die at least twenty times before you came in the room. Each time his body fell a piece of my heart broke. Looking at you right now is killing me, Zeke. Looking into your eyes pains me because all I see is Liam dying." Eniko went and fell back on the bed still crying. I just stood there because I didn't know what to say. I was fighting for a person that was never going to see me as the person I am. Eniko was only going to see me as the person responsible for Liam's death. How the fuck was I supposed to be with her when she only saw the worse in me?

I went over to the bed and laid next to her not saying nothing. Her soft cries pained my ears. I wanted to fix this I just didn't know how. I didn't even know who the fuck made the tape. That shit happened two years ago and the only people who knew about it was, Haze, Drix, Liam, and I. Liam was dead so there wasn't no way that nigga could've been talking from the grave. Haze was my cousin and doing bitch shit just wasn't in his blood, leaving Drix as the person who could've done it.

That nigga could've done the shit because he was feeling salty about me putting my hands on him because of that shit with Macy. That was the only logically explanation and the more I thought about it the more murder crossed my mind.

"Let's go," I told Eniko getting up from the bed.

"Zeke, I don't want to go nowhere with you!" she sobbed.

"You don't got a fucking choice, Eniko. I drove you out here now let's go."

"Just bring me home and then you can be out of my life for good," she said slowly getting off the bed.

I didn't say shit to her, I just held her hand as I brought her back out to my car. I wasn't the type to assume shit, I was heading straight to Drix to find out if he was behind this fuck shit. I had nothing but love for that nigga and I would hate to have to kill my brother behind some bitch shit.

## *18: Emanii*

"When you gonna stop giving me the cold shoulder, Manii? You know I didn't mean to put my hands on you."

Drix and I were still at odds and it was going to be like this for a while. I wasn't about to just forgive his ass because he been bringing me gifts and flowers. That shit didn't mean anything to me and everything he was buying for me I could buy myself or have Haze or Zeke buy it for me. What Drix did to me was something I never thought he would ever do, so to make sure he didn't do it again I was going to make him suffer.

"I'm not giving you the cold shoulder. I still talk to you when you speak to me; I still cook, and make sure that you have clean clothes and a clean house to come home to."

"Yeah but we're not how we used to be, Manii. Just tell me what I can do to make things better."

"I don't know what you can do to make things better but I can tell you what I'm going to do to make things better. Since you putting your hands on me came about because I told you I wanted to Columbia and you thought it was such a problem, I decided to go ahead and accept their offer. It's a full ride and that's something I just can't see myself turning down. You think I can't do it so I'm going to prove to you that I can."

"Ight if that's what you want to do then I'll support you a hundred percent."

"Why couldn't you just support me a hundred percent when I brought it up to you, Hendrix?"

"I don't know, Emanii. I know how much going to school means to you and I also know how you get when things get a little stressful. I just didn't want you feeling no type of way towards our baby. That's my fault though because I shouldn't put my mother issues off on you because your nothing like her."

"Thank you for that because you're right I'm nothing like your mother and I never will be. Me going to school just isn't for me, it's for my baby too. I don't care that I'm pregnant at eighteen, I refuse to become a statistic and I refuse for my child to grow up knowing his mother is a statistic. This hustling shit isn't going to last forever and I'm not okay with just depending on you to provide for me. I'm a smart girl and I plan on using my smarts to get me somewhere."

"I hear you, Manii. I'm gonna be here with you every step of the way. I love you girl." He scooped me into his arms and kissed me so passionately that I started leaking.

"Oh you missed me, huh?" he moaned into my mouth.

"Something like that," I giggled.

"Wassup, you trying to throw it back?"

"Nope, just because we cool doesn't mean you are getting any play boy. I will be using my toy tonight." I pushed him away from me then stood up laughing.

"Don't play with me, Manii."

"I'm not playing, Hendrix. I'm serious no nooky for you tonight boo."

"Ma, I'll take that shit if I have to. A nigga's been missing you for a week."

"And you're gonna continue missing me for another week. Now get the door." I went into the kitchen leaving him to answer the door. It was eight at night so someone knocking on the door wasn't out of the usually. I knew Zeke was with Eniko having dinner so that only left Haze. I haven't seen much of him since the block party, according to Macy they been having a fuck marathon. She seemed happy so I was happy for my girl. Her and Haze were so much a like that I knew it was only going to be a matter of time before they found their way back to each other.

"Zeke, the fuck is you doing, my nigga?" I heard Drix yell. I stopped pouring a glass of water and rushed back into the living room. Both Drix and Zeke had their guns out pointed at the other. I was at a loss for words and didn't know who to tell to put their gun down first.

"What is going on?" I managed to say. Eniko was standing against the wall crying and mumbling he's dead, as if the scene that was going on didn't faze her at all.

"Ask your brother, I answer the door and this nigga gonna pull a gun on me. Zeke, I let you get that hit off because I deserved that shit. I'm not about to keep letting you punk me. You're definitely not going to punk me in my own fucking home," Drix gritted. Drix getting upset was very rare but when he did, he would start grinding his teeth. Usually when he did that things weren't going to end too well.

"Zeke, what is going on? Why are you here and why is Eniko crying?" I asked.

"Just answer this question for me, Drix. You my man so I'm going to give yo ass the benefit of the doubt."

"Give me the benefit of the doubt for what I ain't fucking do shit, my nigga."

"Did you make a fucking video of Liam's death and have that shit playing at my house."

"The fuck did you just say?" Drix asked him, cocking his gun back.

"Hendrix no, just put the gun down that's my brother!" I yelled. I moved closer to where they were but not too close because I wasn't stupid.

"Nigga, you heard what the fuck I said. Did you record that shit?"

"How the fuck was I supposed to record that shit when I was the one driving the fucking car? Liam was my nigga just as well as he was yours, what makes you think I would do some fucked up shit like that?"

"Ayo, Manii, why you're front...Yo what the hell is going on?" Haze yelled walking in the house along with Macy behind him. Macy ran over to where Eniko was and held her while trying to ask her what was wrong.

"This nigga came up in here with his gun out asking me if I recorded Liam dying then set the shit up at his house," Drix explained.

"Zeke, you didn't do that shit did you my nigga?" Haze asked him.

"We were the only ones fucking there who else would've recorded that shit. The fucking video was playing in my fucking house Haze. Eniko seen that shit and it was playing on repeat."

"I don't know who the fuck did that shit but I know it wasn't Drix. That nigga don't even move funny to do no shit like that. Come on man we been friends for ten plus years, put the fucking guns down. We got bigger shit to talk about."

Drix and Zeke put their guns down but didn't put them away. I walked over to where they were and smacked the shit out of the both of them.

"Ezekiel you are my brother and Hendrix you are my damn boyfriend. Did either one of you think how I would feel seeing the two of you having guns pointed at each other. I am damn near six months pregnant, are the two of you trying to send me into premature labor?" I rolled my eyes at the both of them then smack the shit out of Haze too.

"Manii, I didn't even do shit," Haze complained.

"I haven't seen your ass since the block party. I'm going to need you to stop keeping my girl hostage before she ends up like me. I'm going to take Eniko and Macy into my room. By the time I come back out I want the three of you to fix whatever bullshit y'all got going on."

I glared at each and every one of them so they knew I was serious. I didn't know what was going on but it felt like I was starting to become the mother hen of the group. We were all back together and the drama just kept coming. The day that we were all on the same page and things were back to normal was a day that I wish would come soon. I helped Macy as best as I could carry Eniko into my bedroom. We sat her on the bed as she continued to cry. I looked at Macy and she just shrugged her shoulders.

"Eniko, what is wrong mama?" I asked, sitting down on the bed. This baby was kicking already and my body was just overall tired.

"I saw him die. I watched his body fall to the ground over and over again," she mumbled.

"Eniko, I know that it hurts but you can't keep dwelling on it. Dwelling on it is only going to make it worse," Macy said, climbing on the other side of the bed.

"Macy is right, Eniko. The more you think about it the worse you are going to feel."

"I know but how am I supposed to get passed it? Zeke and I were finally going to work on being a couple when I saw the video. When I look into his eyes I see Liam being murdered." She sniffled.

"You are going to get passed it because you have me and Macy by your side. We will help you work through this

Eniko but what you can't do is blame Zeke for what happened. He didn't set the video up for you to see and he didn't set up Liam to die. You're not the only who struggled with Liam's death. We all did but Zeke took it the hardest. He started an annual cookout in the name of Liam just to help him cope with the pain. I'm sure Zeke seeing the video hurt him as well. The both of you need each other because if anyone is going to understand how either one of y'all feel it's going to be the y'all. Stop pushing my brother away, Eniko because all you're doing is making up excuses for you not to be with him."

"Yeah, Manii is right. I know I told you to date both Zeke and Gavin but I honestly feel like Zeke is who you should be with. Give him a chance and stop allowing the fear of the unknown bother you."

Even though this wasn't the right time I was happy that I had both of my girls back in my life. Conversations like this is what I missed when they left. I didn't have anyone to really bond with and now that they were back I wasn't going to let them go. I didn't care if they moved to Alaska I was going to move right with their asses because things just didn't feel right when we weren't together.

Macy and I continued giving Eniko advice on how to get over what she had to see tonight. I was confused as hell that someone videotaped what happen and decided tonight of all nights to reveal that there was a tape. I didn't know who exactly went through all that trouble but I knew when it came to the light who they were death was going to be their fate. Zeke played about a lot of things but the one thing he didn't play with was the people he cared about. When it came to the people he cared about he would go above and beyond for them even if it meant killing someone in the process.

## *19: Hendrix*

"Ight this silent shit is for the birds. Someone better say something so we can put this shit behind us!" Haze spat.

For the past thirty minutes we have been sitting here in silence. I had too much pride to say anything to Zeke after that shit he just pulled. If he wasn't Manii's brother I would've deaded his ass because what he did tonight broke the bro code. I wasn't just some random nigga in the streets. Zeke and I have known each other for over ten years and he thought he could just come up in my house and pull a gun out on me because of some bullshit.

"I don't got shit to say cause this nigga should've known better. How the fuck could you think I would film Liam's death, then sneak into your house, and play that shit? I'm not even that type of nigga," I gritted.

"Shit, I thought you weren't the type of nigga to hit my sister and you did that shit."

"Nigga, you funny right now. That shit was a mistake and you know that shit."

"Ight this shit ain't getting nowhere and we got more important shit to talk about. Both of y'all were wrong for what the fuck I walked into. Zeke, Drix is your boy and you know him better than that. He would never do no shit like that and you know it. Drix you were wrong for pulling a gun out on this nigga because you know how fucked up he felt when Liam died."

"So cause this nigga wanted to be in his fucking feelings I should've just let him have a gun pointed in my face like I'm some bitch. The nigga came in my house being disrespectful, not the other fucking way around."

"You know this nigga wasn't going to shoot you, you are the father of his sister's baby. Zeke maybe a lot of things but one thing he's not is dumb. He would never kill you off the strength of Manii."

"I don't want to hear that shit. If things were the other way around you would be pissed the fuck off too, Haze."

"I never said I wouldn't but I wouldn't drag the shit either. We got a nigga we don't even know gunning for us and the two of y'all want to be bitchin' about some shit that we can figure out later. For all we know the nigga that's trying to get at us is the person who filmed the shit and set you up Zeke."

"How the fuck could that nigga have filmed it? You mean to tell us that we had beef with a nigga for two fucking years and we just finding out? That shit don't even sound legit," Zeke told Haze.

"What nigga are y'all talking about?"

Since Zeke the block party, I haven't been really kicking it with Haze and Zeke. The only time we talked was when it had to do with business. Other than that I wouldn't say shit to either one of them. I knew they were feeling some type of way about me putting my hands on Emanii, so I was trying to give them their space.

"We ran up on that bitch nigga Macy was fucking with and let's just say that the nigga had one up on us," Haze said, shaking his head.

"Had one up on y'all, how?"

"The nigga had shooters somewhere in the area because out of nowhere we had red dots on us. Mind you we were in Macy's old house so that shit had to be coming from somewhere close. But she got so many fucking windows in her living room it was hard to tell which direction they came from," Zeke explained.

"That's what you should've been coming here to tell me instead of that bullshit. When we riding out?" I asked.

"We can't ride out because we don't know what the fuck we up against. I dumped Macy's car cause she said from the way the nigga was talking that he had been watching her."

"Has any one hit up Dean? How we know this shit isn't another fucking test?"

"Why would that nigga be testing us?" Zeke asked.

"He wants us to become his new distros it only makes sense. He was the one who told us to kill that nigga Big L. From the way I'm looking at shit everything points to that nigga."

"Now that you saying that shit aloud that makes sense. Haze call that nigga up and tell him we need a meeting right fucking now," Zeke said.

"You don't even got to say it, I'm already dialing."

"Yo my bad Drix. I was trying to do something nice for Eniko to show her that we could be great together and shit. Everything was going smooth until she seen that video. I wasn't thinking straight, all I was thinking about was someone fucking up what I had going with Eniko. The thought that Eniko and I could be over before we even really began clouded my thinking."

"You don't got to explain because I get it. We cool." We gave each other a brotherly hug then dapped each other up.

"It's about time y'all kissed and made up." Haze laughed.

"Aren't you supposed to be calling that nigga Dean, mind yo business, my nigga," I joked.

"His ass ain't answering the phone; he's looking real guilty in my eyes. Zeke, you call that nigga and see if he picks up."

"Ight." Zeke pulled out his phone dialed the number then put it on speaker.

The phone kept ringing and ringing. From the looks of things Dean was the nigga behind everything. He was our connect and all but even the connect had to die for being disloyal. In my eyes no one was above death when it came to certain shit.

"Speak," Dean said into the phone.

"Yo where you at we need to have a meeting." Zeke told him.

"I'm kind of tied up at the moment—"

"Nigga, you tied up and we got questions that need answers. We either meeting tonight or you can kiss our business goodbye!" I spat. I didn't have time of the run around bullshit Dean was doing. I had a baby on the way and I needed to know if niggas were really gunning for us or was this just another test.

We could hear Dean talking to someone in the background but couldn't make out what was being said.

"Okay, from the sound of your voice I can tell that this is urgent. I'm not currently in New York right now so if the meeting has to go down tonight I'm going to need y'all to drive out to Philly."

"What's the address?" Haze asked.

"I'll text to you when you are an hour out of New York."

"Ight," Zeke said, hanging up the phone. "I think that nigga is playing games," he told us.

"I'm not trusting that nigga too much either," Haze agreed.

"We may not trust that nigga but we taking that ride to Philly. I need answers, we just gonna have to be strapped up and ready for whatever," I told them.

"Fuck it let's go," Haze said.

"I'm not leaving the girls here though they gonna have to follow us to Philly or some shit," Zeke said.

"We can take my truck and all ride together. I don't feel right letting them drive in a separate car. We don't know who are enemies are right now, the only way to keep them safe is to keep them close."

"That nigga has a point."

"Ight, I'm going to send Manii and Macy out here so y'all can tell them wassup. I need to talk to Eniko about some shit. I was gonna keep all this shit away from her, but if we bringing them with us I'm gonna need her to know what's going on."

"Just make that shit fast so we can go. I don't want to give that nigga Dean too much time to try some shit if he is shiesty," I told Zeke.

Two minutes after Zeke went to the back Macy and Manii came into the living room. I explained to Manii what was going on and just like I knew she would she was down to ride. With her being pregnant I didn't really feel too safe having her wait out in the car while we met with Dean, but I also didn't trust her ass being anywhere without me. I wasn't going to let Manii out of my sight until we found out what was going on. I would die before I allow anything to happen to my unborn child and Manii. They were my life and I would trade my life just so they could keep theirs.

## *20: Eniko*

"You ight in here?" Zeke asked, pulling me on to his lap.

"I don't know if I'm okay but I'm sure I will be sooner than later," I told him.

"You know I didn't have anything to do with that tape, right?"

"I know." I was still upset behind seeing Liam's death on that tape but I knew I couldn't punish Zeke for it. Deep down I knew he had nothing to do with it, I only blamed him because I wanted a reason to not be with him.

"I swear on everything I'm going to find out who did that shit and when I do it's lights out for them, Eniko."

"Stop Zeke, you can't solve every issue with murder. Maybe me seeing that video was something that I needed to see."

"How could you seeing that be something that you needed to see, Eniko? That shit was foul and the person who fucking did it deserves to die. I don't give a fuck what you say, this is gonna be a problem that's solved with death."

"I needed to see it because it made me realize that I've been using Liam's death to push you away. I knew since I saw you in Geno's that we were going to somehow find our way back to each other. I knew because you looked at me the same way you did when we shared our first kiss. You looked at me and our connection could be felt throughout the room even with the chaos that was going on at the time. My heart went flat when Liam died, and when I saw you again it started beating. I knew that with you was where I wanted to be I was just too scared to take it there. So I used the fact that you were Liam's friend and him dead as a reason to not mess with you.

Then today I was ready to give you a chance I was ready to step out on faith and see if the connection I felt was something real. I was ready but then I saw the video and that changed everything for me. It was reminder that the life you are in can take your life the same it did Liam's. When Liam died I went into a dark hole, I didn't think I was ever going to be able to crawl out but somehow I did. If I lose you Zeeky, I'm not sure I will make it out."

"Eniko, you don't have to ever worry about making it out of that dark hole again because I'm never going anywhere. I'm too stubborn to die and refuse to leave you alone on this earth. I'm gonna always be here for you whether it's in friendship or as your man. You stuck with me for life, ma." he told me.

The sincerity that was in his eyes made it hard not to melt in his arms. I was tired of fighting what I felt for Zeke. With watery eyes and tear stained cheeks I grabbed his face and kiss him the same way I kissed him when we shared our first kiss. Having his hands rubbing over my body and our lips touching caused my body to come alive. I pushed him back and straddled him ready to give him access to my exclusive club.

"Chill out Eniko we can't do that right now. As bad as I want to, I can't."

"Why because we in your sister's room?" I asked confused. He didn't have an issue with giving me head in his sister's bathroom so why did he have an issue now?

"We got to take a ride out to Philly. Some strange shit is happening and we need to meet with our connect to see if he has something to do with it or if this is all because of that Rex nigga."

"Wait what does Rex have to do with this."

Zeke gave me the run down on what happened earlier with Rex. I was shocked because Rex didn't seem that well connected. Yeah, he was street dude but he always moved by himself. I never seen him with anyone other than Gavin.

"Okay so you are going to Philly why do I have to come?"

"I'm not leaving you in New York unprotected. That nigga Rex has eyes on Macy which means that Gavin could've had eyes on you too. I'm not taking any chances."

"Gavin doesn't even hustle," I told him.

"Yeah, I don't trust that shit. What nigga hangs with a dude that hustles that doesn't hustle himself?"

"I'm telling you if anyone has anything to do with what's going on I really doubt it's Gavin."

"You sticking up for the nigga? Or do you just know him that well?" Zeke asked me.

"I'm just saying. We have chilled a couple of times and he is as regular as regular comes."

"Look that nigga could've told you what you wanted to hear just to fuck with you. You sticking up for the nigga isn't going to change how I feel about dude. I don't trust that nigga nor am I leaving you out here alone."

"Fine," I told him.

"That's my girl." He leaned in giving me a kiss then stood up. "Aye, since you mine now the only nigga you defend is me. I don't want you to hear you sticking yo neck out for other nigga that isn't me. I don't like that shit."

"Someone sounds jealous," I joked.

"Call it what you want, just make sure you don't do the shit again. Here take your phone," he said, tossing it to me.

I laughed at Zeke as we left out the room because he may not have wanted to say it but his ass was jealous. No matter what Zeke said I didn't believe that Gavin had anything to do with what was going on because it just wasn't in his nature. He seemed too laid back to try and kill someone. I pulled my phone out and sent Gavin a text letting him know that I needed to talk to him. I wasn't just going to sit and wait for Zeke to figure things out. Since we were going to Philly I planned on sneaking off to go and meet Gavin to find out what was going on. Gavin hit me right back saying he would meet me in the morning and we could have breakfast together. My conscious wasn't going to allow me to just sit back and allow Zeke to kill someone who might potentially be innocent. I couldn't save Liam so I was going to try and save Gavin because I honestly believed he didn't have anything to do with this.

## 21: Macy

"Why do all three of you have to go inside. I don't feel safe staying out here in the car. Manii is pregnant and Eniko is Eniko," I told Haze. It was around two in the morning and it was dark as hell outside. We were sitting outside of a warehouse and the whole scene was just creepy.

"What does Eniko is Eniko supposed to mean?" She asked.

"Exactly what it sounds like. You and I don't know nothing about this street shit. I don't wanna get got."

"Macy is right. Why not have the meeting outside. That way if something seems off we can help y'all or at least hold the doors open for y'all to jump in and we can go." Manii said.

"How are the three of you going to help us?" Haze questioned.

"Give us guns," I said.

"You just said we don't know anything about this street stuff yet you want them to give us guns," Eniko said.

"It can't be that hard, what do you do just aim and pull the trigger?" I asked.

"That shit don't sound like a bad idea. We don't know what we are about to walk into. Having the meeting out here might give us a better advantage if the nigga is playing dirty," Haze said. Now wasn't the time to be thinking this but I couldn't help but to smile at how thugged out and fine Haze looked. I was scared and excited at the same time, if we walked away from this alive I was gonna put it on him in the worse way.

"Manii, you take the gun in the glove compartment and Macy you use this one. Eniko, I'm not givin' you nothin' cause I don't need you shooting anyone by accident and shit," Zeke said. "Let me call this nigga and tell him to come out." Zeke leaned over gave Eniko a kiss then hoped out the car.

"Hold the gun with two hands to get it as steady as you can. When you are ready to shoot make sure that the safety is off. Once you're sure it's off aim and then pull the trigger," Haze told me. "Be careful ma cause I don't need you getting hurt."

"Don't worry about me I got this. Just make sure that you get back in this car in one piece."

"You really don't know how much a nigga has changed do you?" He laughed.

"I don't but I would like to find out so be careful, Haze." I gave him a kiss and then he jumped out the van. Drix said a few words to Emanii kissed her then left out the van leaving us alone.

"I need the two of you to cover for me when we leave here," Eniko said whispering. I was trying to keep my eyes on Haze but she kept repeating the same sentence over and over.

"Why do you need us to cover for you?" Manii asked never taking her eyes off of Drix.

"Zeke told me what happened with Rex and for some reason he feels like Gavin has something to do with it too."

"Okay, so why are you meeting up with him? I'm lost." I asked.

"I need to talk to him to see if he has anything to do with it. I can't just let Zeke kill an innocent man especially after what happened with Liam."

"I understand what you're saying but I don't think it's a good idea," Manii told her, shaking her head.

"Yeah neither do I. What if he does have something to do with this and he snatches you for a ransom or even worse kills you."

"Gavin wouldn't do that," she said, sounding so sure.

"Eniko, how do you know what he would and wouldn't do? You have only been talking to him for like a month."

"You can learn a lot about someone in a month—"

"Okay we can talk about this later. Look, two guys are coming out of the warehouse." Manii said, interrupting Eniko.

I was glad Manii changed the subject because if Eniko would've kept going then we probably would've ended up fighting. There wasn't no way I was covering for her so she could go and do some bullshit like that. I didn't trust Gavin because he was too close to Rex and Rex was on some other shit. I planned on telling Zeke all about Eniko's plan just to keep her ass safe.

Looking out the window I could see Haze going on off on one of the men. I was squinting my eyes trying to get a better look at who the man was but it was too dark out.

"I wonder what Haze is going off about?" Manii asked.

"I don't know but it looks like…oh shit, who the fuck is this?"

Out of nowhere a black Lexus came speeding up with their headlights on. A woman got out the car with a bat in her hand.

"MOM!" Eniko yelled, getting out of the truck. I ran after her but stopped in my tracks when I saw who Haze was going off on.

"Mom, what are you doing here?" Eniko yelled.

"Erin, what are you doing here?" the man asked, looking at her with a shocked expression on his face. Erin was crying and shouting something as she swung her bat wildly. Everyone was so caught up in Erin that no one noticed me walking up. I still had the gun Haze gave me in my trembling hands. The closer I got the more I could feel my heart being ripped out of my body.

"PLEASE TELL ME THIS IS A MISTAKE!" I yelled, grabbing everyone's attention.

"Macy, what are you doing here?"

"NO DAD, TELL ME WHAT ARE YOU DOING HERE?" I screamed back. Tears were streaming down my face and snot was running from my nose but I didn't care because I needed fucking answers.

"YO DAD IS THE NIGGA WE'VE BEEN WORKING FOR THIS WHOLE FUCKING TIME. THE SAME NIGGA THAT TOOK YOU AWAY FROM ME FOR BEING A STREET NIGGA IS THE MAN THAT

EMPLOYEED ME INTO THE GAME!" Haze gritted, standing next to me.

"Baby, let me explain. Erin, put the bat down and chill out," my father said.

"FUCK YOU, MARTIN!" Erin yelled.

I stood there wondering how my father could judge Haze for hustling when this nigga was the fucking connect. I didn't understand what was going on, and I didn't want to understand the scene that was in front of me. All I knew is that I wanted him to hurt, I wanted him to feel the same pain I felt when he took me away from Haze. I raised my gun, with my hands sweaty and trembling. There was so much commotion going on around me that I couldn't concentrate on what I was trying to. I tried to steady my hand but I couldn't.

The guy who was standing next to my father was the first body to drop, followed by Eniko's body. Erin's screams drowned out the sound of the gun shots as my father's body was the next to drop. My hands were still trembling as I stood there listening to Erin cry and asking God why. Gunshots and cries were the only thing I could hear as I made my way over to my father's body. I didn't feel an ounce of remorse as I stood there watching blood seep out of his mouth. My body turned cold as stood there watching his life slip away from his body.

# *To Be Continued...*

## *Other Books by Kellz Kimberly*

Falling for a Real Nigga 1-4

A Player's Prayer (Standalone Novel)

Gunz & Laci: Black Rose Mafia (Standalone Novel)

He Got Me in My Feelings 1& 2

Lay My Heart on The Line for You 1&2

She Gotta be the Dopest to Ride with the Coldest 1&2

Made in the USA
San Bernardino, CA
25 March 2017